LISA MICHELLE

FOREST CREEK

BOOKS

Vinci Books

vinci-books.com

Published by Vinci Books Ltd in 2025

1

Paperback ISBN: 9781036707187

By Lisa Michelle

Calaveras Crime

Blue Mountain
Calaveras
Forest Creek

For Sarah Mizhir
And all who have disappeared deep in the wilderness,
I'm forever sorry I couldn't save you.

*There is a savage beast in every woman
who stirs when you put a sword in her hand
and wakes with the scent of blood.*

PART I
Chapter One

September 23

Under a harvest moon the color of fire, I entered the burn scar naked and black and frigid as the night. All because I refused to die. Refused to accept the convenience of a peaceful death. It was not luck or sk ill that brought me this far. It was the same willpower I had fed my patients for years. Feeding it to myself was rare, but now a matter of life or death. Conjuring elusive willpower, it turned out, was grueling and teetering on the precipice of irrational as hypothermia swallowed me whole.

Darkness came the moment my bleeding feet stepped into Forest Creek.

"Fate." My breath clouded, reminding me I was still alive and shivering.

"Kismet." I moved primal—graceful—deeper into the urgent and complicated current. Its blathering rumbled my head like a nightmare, but all too real.

The shivering ceased.

"Destiny." Water splashed my thighs. Up my torso into a numbing heat like nothing I'd ever felt before. There was no cold left in me. Stumbling over rocks tainted with slick algae, I fell. My hands buried in the viscous bottom, face to face with the bruised and beaten stranger in the water. Staring deep into her orbs—to see what darkness hid under the surface.

"Liar," she whispered.

I crawled away from her, into the shallows, as the creek rambled on—an endless rhapsody of nothing in particular, like my overdramatic patients. All of them like water, running from something in the past. I'd lost track of time and fumbled from the creek. Willingly, into the cauterized world, where trees cast bony shadows in moonlight.

The forest suffered from motley shades of black. Year-old smoke and the essence of charred remains carried a tinge of sweetness. On my hands and knees, but unable to recall the moment I'd succumbed to crawling. Slowly. My long limbs like a praying mantis stalking her lover. Ravens followed. Watching. Awaiting sunrise to pluck out my eyes should I quit. Their sharp beaks pecking holes in my flesh. Holes in my story. Past the bone, down to the marrow. To the real me, before the world told me who to be.

I moved toward the improbable warmth of scorched earth until it gave way to a massive hole. A stump hole. The remains of a monstrous pine which had burned and sunk to ash. Heat like open arms drew me in and I burrowed myself deep inside the blackened den. Ashes to ashes, dust to dust. And earth as soft as a silk cocoon. In the fetal position, my soul found repose. I closed my eyes and drifted away until I saw the light.

September 22

The day before, I'd awoken to a lengthy state of hypnopompic hallucinations and lingered there a while. The vivid visions had come and gone, for no diagnosable reason, since I was a little girl. There is no cure and the hallucinations are not associated with mental illness. I'd learned long ago to encourage and explore the hypnopompic state, as did Thomas Edison, Isaac Newton, Nikola Tesla, and Beethoven. While in a relaxed but focused consciousness, the brain is highly suggestible and prone to creativity and problem solving. Morning hallucinations rarely appeared, but when they did, were an insightful gift.

It was the first day of fall and my last chance to fish before the season closed. I skipped the caffeinated green tea and obtained my wake-up jolt from cold water therapy in the shower. It was like pressing reset, a sort of Control-Alt-Delete on my body. After thirty seconds of focused breathing, the frigid temperature no longer felt threatening. Mind and body quit resisting. The exhilaration would last for hours. One month of daily cold therapy, and I'd never felt better mentally or physically. I'd worked myself up to enjoying the benefits of a five-minute cold shower.

With my face whitewashed in sunscreen, I threaded my short silver ponytail through a San Francisco Giants ballcap. Spending time in nature untethered pure contentment and I was mindful of the moment—grateful that I had left San Francisco and discovered the treasure of the mountains, rivers, and wildlife.

A grin sprouted as I strapped my helmet on over my cap, added my daypack, and started biking up the trail by sunrise. The long ride uphill seemed easier in the cool of the morning, especially with Walter. The blond mutt was physically fit and ran ahead, bucking with excitement.

By eight that morning, we were nearing the wooden

bridge at Forest Creek. Cowbells chimed from the necks of shiny black mama cows and fat calves stood watering in the creek. Soon the cattle would be gathered and moved to lower country before the first snow. My best friend Kate had convinced me to ride a horse and attempt to assist in their removal last fall. Mostly, I'd been in the wrong place at the wrong time, but with Kate's help I learned the fastest way to move cattle was to slow down.

The herd trotted away, taking cover in the dense woods as Walter and I crossed the bridge. The water level in the creek had dropped since last week, but the pools were deep enough to fish. Crisp morning air carried that spicy scent of autumn and embodied the essence of fly fishing. The solitude and pristine forest had a magical effect on my senses. Some compare it to a rejuvenating religious experience. Days were growing shorter and sunlight exposed the surrounding mountains—transcending tangerine, gold, and red—offering the reassurance that life was as spectacular as it should be.

The old logging roads crisscrossing the mountains were gated and locked, making them off limits to motorized vehicles other than Sierra Pacific Timber Company employees. At the last gate, I dismounted and pushed my bike around the side. Walter went ahead as if he knew the drill and looked back before trotting uphill to a boulder hidden under pine boughs. It was the perfect out of the way place where I'd parked my bike a half-dozen times before. No need to lock it up or worry about it being stolen. Since learning to fly fish last spring, I'd never seen another person here besides Gus, and I hoped I'd run into him today.

August Buller, better known as Gus, had turned out to be one of my favorite patients. Throughout his nineteen years, Gus had been tested and assessed and labeled. His last IQ score equaled seventy, but he was more creative and self-aware than most. When I ran into him near the bridge a few weeks ago, he told me about his gold mining claim. He wanted to strike it rich so he could buy back his parents' buffalo ranch. The plan was to create an animal sanctuary in the little town. "We'll have more animals…than people… Miss Mo," Gus had said with tangible enthusiasm. Miss Mo, he called me, because Maureen and Miss Yamaguchi were both too difficult for him to pronounce. He didn't stammer, but certain words, especially the longer ones, caused hesitation and ultimately frustration. I continued treating Gus even after he turned eighteen, and his visits were no longer covered by the county. Gratis, because his kindness was contagious, and after his sessions, *I* felt better.

Walter sat on the shore, waiting and watching as I worked my fly rod back and forth like a metronome, attempting to perfect the ten and two o'clock with the tip. I became excessive with my false cast until Walter walked away and I released the line. Behind me, the fly hooked in a dogwood tree that had surrendered to fall. Blood red leaves in various stages of death trembled and tumbled to earth as I yanked the line.

"Kuso!" I pulled and pulled downward until the line snapped. The tree kept my last Royal Coachman fly. "Kuso." I'd heard it from my mother. She'd never spoken a word of profanity, but kuso had been her secret way of cursing without actually cursing. It wasn't until I'd completed my thesis on why American men are the most prolific serial killers in the world that I learned what the word meant. My professor called my work kuso, assuming I understood the Japanese word. When I explained I did not, he seemed eager to translate: *"Shit, shit, shit!"*

Controlling frustration was one of the biggest lessons fly

fishing had taught me. That and patience. With a foam ant tied to a new leader, I caught and released six little brook trout. Fishing season would soon end and I wanted to conclude it with a bang. Make each day count. I contemplated for less than a minute before hiking the three-plus miles up the game trail along Forest Creek to fish the honey hole I'd discovered last summer. The wide, deep water sat below a ten-foot waterfall. Last year, I'd caught but didn't land the largest native trout I'd ever seen in the Western Sierra. Water pounded down the silvery granite in spectacular fashion. The honey hole was still as deep and green and perfect as I'd hoped.

When two fish broke the surface and slurped up a mosquito, I gobbled down my peanut butter and honey sandwich, tossed Walter two extra-large Milk Bones, and picked up my rod. Careful to keep my distance so as not allow my shadow to spill out and spook the wild fish, I sent a roll cast across the creek. The fly landed perfectly in a swirl at the edge of the falls. Slowly, the current pulled and bounced the rubber ant toward the far shore. I fed the line and watched the bait bob past a partially submerged cedar. Darker water swallowed the ant. Darker meant deeper. And in theory, deeper meant bigger fish. I narrowed my eyes and focused. My body tensed as I watched the surface. Anxious, I licked my lips and lowered the tip of the rod. Little by little, I stripped in the line.

Fly fishing hadn't been on my radar until one of my patients suggested it. A woman I'll call J.W. had survived a traumatic ordeal at the hands of her veterinarian husband, who'd been prosecuted for killing race horses and making it look as if they'd died of natural causes. The owners collected over a half-million dollars on equine mortality policies. The horrific story evolved into the bestselling novel,

Blue Mountain. They labeled it fiction, but unfortunately it was true.

Before moving to Calaveras County, I had a successful private practice for almost twenty years, until losing my fourth patient to suicide. The young woman had killed her husband and recently given birth to premature twin sons. Shell-shocked, I sold the clinic. The young woman's mother, Kate, and I became each other's sole support. I drove a Prius and she drove a truck. We were opposites in most every way, and neither of us would have survived the loss without the other.

When Kate Callahan returned to her ranch in Calaveras County, she invited me to join her. Said mountain air, chores, and looking after two baby boys wouldn't leave time to mope or fret about the past. The woman is the definition of stoic and typically attempts to conceal kindness with cynicism. Her smile, reserved only for special occasions, cracks the facade, making it impossible not to smile back.

The farmhouse Kate built offered more than enough room and I could not provide a valid reason not to go. After six months, I discovered the lack of behavioral health care services available throughout the county and began accepting new patients once a week on a limited basis. Kate and my new practice pulled me out of the dark corner in which I'd been stuck.

After treating J.W. for the better part of a year, I'd come to admire the woman for surviving hell and coming out the other end stronger than the average mortal. She personified post-traumatic growth. That's why I believed her when she explained how fly fishing could be therapeutic. It made perfect sense. The limbic system of the human brain seeks pleasure and rewards. The feelings are a necessary part of survival. It's the reason people become addicted to drugs.

The first time I caught a fish on a fly rod, I recognized and accepted the addiction, feeding it whenever possible.

The brute snatched the fly and ran, nearly jerking the rod from my grip. Excitement rippled through every kernel of my being. I held my breath. Lifted the rod above my head while keeping the line tight. Give and take—I played the feisty fish and laughed when the brookie thrust itself straight up out of the water and splashed down.

"Ohhh-ho-ho baby!" The rod arched and trembled as I began hand stripping the line. It took skill, and I needed to slow down and think straight like the guide in Montana had taught me last summer, or I'd lose the great trout. "Let the fish run when she must and bring her in when she lets you," he'd said.

By the time the trout neared, I was knee-deep in water. I reached around the fiery red underbelly and cradled her gently enough to twist the barbless hook from her mouth. Sunlight reflected her golden skin and altered it a brilliant mood-ring green. Fins blazed orange, outlined in white and black. An imaginative artist could not have rendered truer beauty. Vibrant blood-red dots freckled her body like stitched beads haloed in sky blue. There was nothing more primitive yet so indescribably beautiful than holding life in the palm of your hand—until I began to overthink and analyze.

Catching a fish caused it fear. Fear gave it strength and the will to fight. A survival mechanism all creatures possess. Harming a fish was the last thing I wanted to do, so what made fishing so exciting? My grandfather had been a fisherman in Japan and he'd shared stories of killing whales, but that only repulsed me. I doubted it had anything to do with genetics. What was the biological lure swaying my human nature? Could I be satisfying something infused into my Homo sapiens DNA from thousands of years ago? That would easily attribute the thrill of fishing to the hunter-gatherer in me, if only I could bring myself to eat what I caught.

"Despite what you may think, there is no such thing as being scared to death, my dear." I lowered the fish into the current. She did not fuss or fight. Content for one magical moment, the trout floated above my hand, until she wasn't.

"Wow." Perfect day—and it was only noon. I'd had enough fishing for today and possibly forever, depending on what my reasons-for-fishing research determined. Also, if I hurried home, there was still time left in the day to work on my manuscript.

The idea for *The Magic Outside Your Comfort Zone* came to me two years ago in an extreme hypnopompic hallucination. I dangled from a rock high above the earth. Cosmic clouds blew by and I'd never been more scared. Looking down at a jagged mountain, I fell. The lucid nightmare of slow-motion falling to my death changed direction and I flew. Filled with a joyous rush of adrenaline, I woke with the sense that I'd been privy to the secret of life and could eat the world. When your subconscious points you in the right direction you'd better listen.

Immediately, I made a list of the things I'd always wanted to do if I could overcome my fears:

Ride a bike. Rock climb. River raft. Hike. Camp. Learn to swim. Smoke a cigar. Skydive. Ride a horse (I'd circled that one because Kate had begged to teach me.) Bungee jump. Zipline. Get a dog! Ride a motorcycle—maybe. Ski. Go on a date (I'd laughed after writing that one.) Try ayahuasca. In capital letters, I wrote, WRITE A BOOK ABOUT THE EXPERIENCE.

I'd spent a year and a half checking off my to-do list and keeping a detailed journal of each experience. The one fear I'd yet to conquer was the dreaded date. I'd sworn off online dating since listening to troubled men seemed too much like work and produced the urge to bill them for my time. One narcissistic oaf thought calling me the Asian Olive Oyl was a compliment. The thought of dating made my palms sweaty and my stomach clench.

After creating a solid outline of my adventures, I'd shared the idea and a rough draft with J.W. The bestselling author liked the way the book might help those unable to conquer their fears and try new things, but she thought it needed a worthy through line to be impactful. It lacked a deep connecting theme to pull the story together and give it meaning. I feared she was correct.

With my fly rod separated into four sections, I stuffed it along with the reel into the side pocket of my daypack and heard Walter barking somewhere off in the distance.

"Walter! Come!" Preoccupied with fishing, I hadn't realized he'd gone. I threw my pack on in a hurry. He barked again. Walter doesn't bark. A clear and present dread prickled my skin.

With the toe of my wet trail runners shoved into a granite crack four feet above my perch, I reached up and took hold of an exposed root and pulled myself up onto the ledge. To my left, the rock offered wonky steps and I scrambled my way through, then climbed up and over another section of granite until I topped the last rock and stepped onto the game trail.

The creek ran at least one hundred feet below. I stood, trying to catch my breath, and called again, "Walter!" Still nothing. I flew down the narrow trail back the way we'd come. Low branches knocked my cap off. I reached down and grabbed it, but was in too much of a hurry to put it on. Walter barked somewhere ahead of me.

"Walter!" I ran with my hat in my hand. Fighting through branches and boughs. Passing the sharp bend in the pathway.

"Walter!" He's never barked at people. It must be a bear, or God forbid, a mountain lion.

"Come here, Walter, come!" I screamed as the trail widened, walled on both sides by manzanita bushes. Running as fast as I could, wishing for bear spray, or the pepper spray Kate had given me. Anything to drive away the threat. Walter's barking became constant and quick. Aggressive and louder. I picked up a heavy stick. Better than nothing.

Walter stood in the middle of the trail, bristled and barking like never before. Something was out there in the brush. Walter stood his ground until a shot rang out.

"Walter!"

My heart sank as Walter yelped and crashed through a wall of manzanita below.

"NO!" I ran to where Walter had stood only a second ago.

The portly dark-haired man wore a camouflage ballcap and a huge black backpack that seemed almost as tall as him. He had wedged himself in the brush and looked at me with a slack and bearded jaw. Rage fueled me.

"You idiot!" I stomped toward him. My hands turned to fists. "You damn idiot!"

The man leveled a silver gun at my face.

I froze.

Lifted my hands in surrender and dropped my cap.

The man shook his head, and his shaggy hair followed. He tried to come at me but seemed stuck. Caught by branches that held him and his giant backpack.

"No, no, no," he said, holding the gun at arm's length as he floundered to break free.

I turned. Ran as hard as I could back the way I'd come. Fully expecting a bullet in my back at any second. Zigzag, I thought, but the path was too narrow. I sprinted by the brushy section. Passed the bend in the trail. Not bothering to duck under low branches, just crashing sideways through them. Ignoring the sting when they slapped and scratched my exposed skin.

Adrenaline coursed as I darted from the trail and moved uphill. Scrambling on all fours up and over one solid piece of granite like a spooked doe. My feet slipping and sliding as I pressed forward. Fingernails breaking and digging at nothing but rock and dirt. Wedged between boulders, I stopped and listened. Nothing but my heart pounding hard in my ears and a heavy breath I fought, but failed to silence.

Crouched, I slid down the backside of the granite and made my way to a forest of thick pine and cedar. Spiderwebs stuck to my sweaty face. Running for my life seemed so unreal. Think ahead—which way, I couldn't decide as I came upon a clear-cut and scanned the surroundings.

"Not going back," I told myself.

"Not downhill. No."

"Forward is too open. He'll see me. Easy target."

"Up. Go up."

I advanced upwards as fast as I could. Past blackened trees like burned matchsticks. It had been almost a year since this section of forest had burned, but the tang of fire lingered. Mountain misery had returned in full and carpeted the ground. My feet tangled and I fell. With legs as heavy as tree stumps, I got up and pressed forward.

Above tree line, I lost the benefit of cover. On an open

slope. East, I thought and looked to the sun for direction. High noon. Useless.

"Kuso!" I allowed instinct to guide me and ran toward the top of the ridge. A shadow to my right caught my eye. I spun. The shadow flew by and I looked up. A red tail hawk circled between clouds, watching me. How I wished I could fly away.

At the top of the ridge, I unzipped the side pocket of my hiking pants. "Please, please, please." I pulled out my cellphone and dialed 911. The call dropped.

"Kuso." I squinted at the signal strength. Zero bars.

Text messages. Sometime texts go through when calls won't. It was worth a try. I pulled up Kate's number and typed. *Man w/gun chasing me @ forest crk! Shot walter! Help.*

I pressed send and worked the phone back into my pocket. Progressing downward at a steep angle, I hoped beyond hope that cutting cross-country would lead me to one of a series of old logging roads.

Time slowed and tangled—stuck somewhere in another dimension. This couldn't be reality. With denial came a second wind and a reassuring sense of calm. Recalling all I'd experienced and survived this past year while scared out of my wits worked like fuel. Energizing me. Days spent running and hiking might save my life.

But what about Walter? Poor Walter. An odd name for a dog, but that was his name when I met him at the animal shelter and who was I to change it? His big monkey eyes looked right through me, begging for nothing more than a little love. I knew the feeling and adopted him. He'd been my adventure partner ever since. Walter proved all dogs are *not* natural swimmers. He struggled in the water more than I did, but together we learned to swim. We'd spent every night together either in a bed or a sleeping bag.

The rescued mutt proved his devotion while camped outside of Glacier National Park. In the middle of the night, I had to pee and crossed paths with a grizzly. All forty-seven pounds of Walter morphed into Cujo. The bristled K-9 refused to back down—willing to give his life to protect the woman he loved. Standing his ground even when the grizzly attempted several false charges. Walter barked until the bear backed down and ran back into the forest. Dogs didn't come any braver or more loyal than Walter. The pain in my heart was as real as the anguish stinging my eyes and blurring the trees below.

Salty tears burned my scratched face, but wind cooled it as I picked up my pace. My pack slapped my back as I ran, jumped, climbed, and slid, descending a steep obstacle course of downed timber and boulders. Steeper terrain lay ahead as I worked my way through an overpopulated forest. Under a thick yet impressive canopy, the day darkened and the temperature dropped. Stray bits of sunlight sliced shadows through trees and turned the ground into prison bars.

An eerie silence turned sinister. A horn blew and my heart lurched until I realized it had come from me. My cell. Someone was calling.

A signal!

I ripped the phone from my pants pocket as I bolted down the hillside and looked at the screen.

KATE CALLAHAN.

Fighting to keep my balance, I pressed the phone to my ear. "Kate! Call the police! There's a man out here and—"

"Hey, lady!" The voice clobbered me like a sucker punch and the world went dark.

Chapter Two

Mo's plea for help, followed by crackling static, ambushed Kate away from her fancy new hydraulic log splitter.

"Mo. Maureen! Hello?" She'd shut the obnoxious engine down before making the call, but still couldn't hear. "Mo!" She pressed the flip phone into her ear and covered the opposite with her palm. Listening for a sign of life. Anything other than the sound of a throbbing pulse filling her ears. Desperate for some sort of clue. What the hell was going on? Who'd be out there with a gun in the middle of the day? And why? None of it made sense.

"Mo!"

Kate had told her, more than a few times, not to go into the woods alone. Mo's response was always the same. "You could come with me." She'd invited Kate on every outing. Even offered to pay her way on a guided rafting trip to Montana. But there wasn't time for fun. Sure, Kate would have loved a vacation. She'd never had one. Running a ranch was a year-round job. Winters were spent feeding cattle. Springtime was for going to market and calving season. Summers were for branding, irrigating, and wildfire protection. Fall was spent preparing for a long cold winter, and now, on top of it all, she had the twins to look after. Not screwing them up had become her number one priority and most likely impossible without Mo. How could she ever explain to the boys about the events that had taken place, the reason their mother took her own life, and why they lived with their grandmother? A time would come when rumors and truths would crush them. The past was always gaining, threatening the death of their innocence, and Kate needed Mo to soften the blow.

Last night when Mo called, she'd begged Kate to join her—reminding her it was fall and that before too long they'd be snowed in. "That's why I need to cut more firewood," had been Kate's response. "I'll buy you a cord of wood," Mo had countered.

"Mo! Can you hear me?" She lifted Joey with one arm and sat him on a stump far from the hot wood splitter. Patrick was busy beating a pinecone with a stick.

The call disconnected. "Fuck," Kate whispered and punched 911. It rang six times—*six*—before an operator answered.

"911. Please hold," a man said.

"No! This is an *emergency!*" Unbridled anger reared up as Kate tried to make sense of being placed on hold when someone's life hung in the balance. "This is fucking nuts. 911 puts people on hold?" She paced with a hand on her hip as Joey rushed from his stump to Patrick and snatched his stick away. Patrick tackled Joey and took him down. The kid's face turned blood-red when he hit the ground. He held his breath until the bawling began.

"What's your emergency?" the operator asked.

Kate covered her free ear with her hand. "My friend is

out at Forest Creek. There's a man with a gun chasing her. He shot her dog and her phone went dead." She tried not to yell, yet be heard over the screaming child.

"Location?" he asked.

"Forest Creek."

"Address?"

Kate lowered her voice. "It's a *creek* out in the forest. It *doesn't have* an address."

"The nearest cross street?"

"Um, Winton Road, I guess. After that it's all Forest Service and Sierra Pacific roads. Spur fifteen would be the nearest access point. But I don't know which way she went or where she was when——"

"Missing person's name?"

"Maureen Yamaguchi. We call her Mo." No one called her Mo until Kate did and Maureen hated the abbreviation. Maureen sounded too rigid and uppity, Kate decided the day they rode out to gather cattle and Maureen's horse ran off with her. Kate yelled, "Whoa, Mo." From then on, despite repeated requests to refrain, Maureen became Mo.

"Your name, ma'am?" the operator asked.

"Kate Callahan." She took a deep breath and tried to calm down.

"Maureen Yamaguchi's age?"

"Fifty-six." She'd be fifty-seven soon. If she lived. The ugly thought impaled itself on reasoning and Kate clamped a hand into her temples.

"Height?"

"I don't know. Five-seven, five-eight. She's tall and skinny with short silver hair. She'll be the one out there running from a man with a fucking gun. *Jesus Christ*, she could be dying right now. Do some goddamn thing!"

"Ma'am, I'm going to need you to take a deep breath

and calm down. Okay?" His words were ridiculously slow as if he were trying to antagonize her. "Can you do that for me?"

"No. This is a waste of time. I got to go." Kate slapped her phone shut knowing that by the time the operator dispatched the call over to the Calaveras Sheriff's Department and they in turn transferred the call to patrol units it would be at least an hour before they'd arrive anywhere near the vicinity.

Instead of wasting more time, she dialed her friend Ed Manetti, whom she'd been sort of dating for almost three years and still refused to admit was her boyfriend, or a friend with benefits, whenever the subject came up. She tried to love him, but it just didn't take. On paper, he was perfect. There was just something missing. She blamed the scars her previous love had left and focused her efforts on grandsons.

"Eddie. Hey, you home?"

"Yeah."

"I need you to come over and get the boys. Please. Mo's in deep shit out at Forest Creek."

Joey stopped crying and mimicked Kate, "Shit, shit, shit, shit." He'd found the old cat curled up in the woodpile.

"Joey, you leave that cat alone! Ed, Mo texted me, a guy with a gun shot Walter and is chasing her. I talked to her for a second before the phone went dead." Kate squeezed the top of her head, then grabbed her mouth when the realization hit her. "Holy shit! Isn't Gus still mining on Forest Creek?" Her nineteen-year-old grandson, Gus, had been working his gold claim all summer. He was probably still there and in danger if there was a man running around with a gun. "I'm pretty sure Gus is camping up there. Can you please watch the boys? I gotta go." Now there were two people to worry about.

"That's not the smartest move, Kate. Some tweaker with a gun out in the woods and you want to go up there?"

"Eddie. I swear to God—if you don't get your ass over here..."

A long silent pause sent Kate's heart spiraling.

"Okay," he sighed, "on my way. I'm hanging up so I can call the sheriff."

"Already called 911 and reported it, but I can get there faster than them."

"See you in ten." He hung up.

It all seemed so unreal. How was this even happening? "Shit."

"Shhhit." Patrick mimicked his brother, and before long the boys were singing the shit song. "Shit, shit, shit."

The boys had turned four and already they cussed because Kate couldn't control her potty mouth. "Stop it, you two."

Since Mo entered her life, Kate had never considered the possibility of not having her in it. Over the last few years, Mo had been her rock. She was more than family or a best friend—she was essential. Mo cured Kate's persistent guilt over her failures as a mother, explained that every one of Kate's decisions to protect her daughter Em came from a place of love—it was a rare and desirable trait. If it weren't for Mo, Kate would still be punishing herself, unable to be the grandmother Patrick and Joey needed. Without Mo's patient love and wisdom, these kids didn't stand a chance. Not having Mo around would be like not breathing.

———

The boys were in the truck when Kate pulled over at her front gate. She got out and waited for Eddie. Each second like nails scratching at her Timex. "Come on." She released her graying side braid and finger-combed the strays back into place. With dirty and calloused fingers, she weaved it tight alongside her neck, as if prepping for battle. Next, she dialed Mo's cellphone over and over without success and paced until Eddie's Subaru came speeding up the dirt road and stopped alongside Kate.

"I called Detective Rocha and left him a message," he said as he got out of his car. "I also spoke to CHP in Sacramento for a helicopter, but they're fogged in. Everything's grounded."

"Of course it is. Shit." Kate lifted Joey out of her truck and set him in the back of Eddie's car. "I'll call Danny K. He knows that area better than anyone." Danny Kilpatrick had patrolled for the Forest Service as long as Kate could remember. Fondly known by locals and old timers as Danny K. he would likely be more help than the sheriff's department. Joey squirmed as Kate buckled him in, although they'd only be driving on the ranch back to Kate's house.

Eddie moved Patrick from the pickup to his car. "When I explained the situation to CHP, she surmised the man chasing Mo is most likely a grower. I know there's no point in telling you how dangerous this is and that you shouldn't be going, but it's harvest season and these bastards won't jeopardize losing everything they worked for to a bust."

"And I'm not gonna jeopardize Mo."

"I'm not asking you to. I'm asking you to consider the possibility of who you may be dealing with. They shot two hunters dead up in Siskiyou the other day."

"Hunters." The idea was a momentary reprieve.

"Maybe it was a hunter." Kate wanted to convince herself more than Eddie.

"Why would a hunter be chasing her?" he asked.

"He shot her dog and…" Kate did her best to create a plausible explanation. "I don't fucking know. He's a psycho who didn't get his buck. Maybe he was poaching…and on meth. You know how paranoid tweakers can get."

"You're grasping. But okay, so going after Mo with a psycho hunter on meth is so much safer?" He shook his head.

Kate fought the buckle on Joey's car seat. "Fu…dge."

"It's fine. You think I'm going to get in a wreck going up the driveway?"

Kate gave up. "Thought when Prop 64 passed we'd be rid of all the illegal growing." Kate kissed Joey. "I love you." Then she leaned across the seat and kissed Patrick. "I love you. You guys be good for Eddie okay?"

"Kay." Patrick nodded as Joey kicked at the back of the driver's seat. Kate tried one last time to buckle Joey into his car seat. It slid in, grabbed with a click, and gave Kate an odd sense of satisfaction and security. She did the best she could. Didn't just give up because it was a little difficult. She shut the door and admired the beautiful boys, hoping to hell she and Mo would be back in time for dinner with them.

"I just read an article in the L.A. Times—according to US Drug Enforcement there are more pot farms growing illegally on federal land than prior to legalizing it in 2016." Eddie followed Kate to her truck. "They're profiting millions."

"Wouldn't it be easier to just grow legally?"

"No way. Growers can avoid paying a fortune in licensing and taxes, and—they don't need to buy property. Just find an isolated spot in the forest, which isn't difficult, and set up shop. DEA and law enforcement are over-whelmed with fentanyl and methamphetamines. If they do bust an illegal grow site, they seldom make an arrest, so the son of a bitches are right back at it in a week or two." Eddie hadn't taken a breath. His red face proved he needed a moment to settle down. Catch his breath. Perhaps the fun facts would force Kate to reconsider. She knew how he operated. He was a lawyer for Christ's sake.

"Nice closing argument. I gotta go." Kate opened the truck door.

"*Please* wait for the sheriff."

She turned and faced him. "You know as well as I do they won't get serious about finding her until tomorrow morning. No way they're gonna search in the dark. If it were me out there, I sure hope someone would come to help. I know Mo would."

"You can't stop a bullet, Kate."

She raised an eyebrow, tilted her head, and rolled her eyes.

"This may sound harsh, Kate, but think of the person who jumps into a raging river to save someone—*they both* usually end up drowning."

"I ain't the type to stand by and watch someone drown. Neither is Mo. Her kind doesn't come around every day." Kate jumped into her truck. "If I ain't back by dark, call Roper. He can feed and water the animals."

"The boys and I will do. Please be careful." He leaned in and kissed her. Without thinking, she wiped her lips with the back of her hand.

"There's leftovers in the fridge." She pulled the door, then stopped halfway. "Thanks." She shut the door.

Eddie shook his head as Kate drove away watching him in the rearview. She sped onto the main road that passed a variety of offshoot red dirt logging roads. Spur Fifteen was four miles uphill—back and forth on partially paved curves. Before losing cell service, Kate pulled up Danny Kilpatrick's number and called him.

"This is Dan Kilpatrick with the US Forest Service Patrol—leave a message and I'll call you back just as soon as the cellular service allows. Have a great day." He sounded like a commercial for used cars.

"Danny, hey, this is Kate Callahan. My friend Maureen is up at Forest Creek and called saying a man shot her dog and was chasing her. Something bad is going down. I'm heading to Spur Fifteen and need your help. I won't have service in a minute, so just come on…and please hurry." She clapped her phone shut and tossed it in the cup-holder.

The last few years with Mo as roommate had been a blessing. Having an honest friend who called you out when you were burying yourself with bullshit had been a tiny miracle. Little things, like saying good night at the end of each day and good morning with a steaming cup of coffee fixed exactly the way Kate liked it. Hazelnut creamer with a splash of heavy whipping cream topped with a dash of cinnamon. No one had ever cared enough to bring Kate coffee, let alone concoct it correctly. Kate could see with the chance of losing Mo that she had made another huge mistake when she let Mo get her own place. Kate hammered the steering wheel with her fist. "Fuuuck!"

The green metal gate at Spur Fifteen was closed. "God-damn it." Kate squeezed the steering wheel as she thought about ramming her truck through and busting the chain. Instead, she stopped, and got out hoping it was only dummy locked. It wasn't. Nothing was ever that easy. The clock that might be Mo's life ticked down in Kate's mind. She couldn't shake the possibility of Mo taking her last breath at that very moment. There wasn't time to consider options.

Kate jumped in her truck, backed it up, and floored the gas pedal. She hit the gate doing thirty. It sprang so hard and fast that it bounced back and ripped off the driver's side mirror.

Forty miles an hour on a red dirt road left little room for error. If a deer, or a cow, or any critter crossed her path, it would be unfortunate for them both. A dust cloud flamed behind Kate for three miles until she arrived at the second gate and stopped. She parked in the road, as Danny K. unloaded a four-wheeler off the back of his green Forest Service truck. How the hell did he get here so fast, was her first thought.

Kate stepped out and walked over.

"Kate. Hi. How are you?" Danny had one of those goofy, overbite, Howdy Doody smiles so big it lit up his entire freckled face. His head was as clean-shaven as his face. A slight lisp and rosy cheeks gave him a youthful appearance, although he was closer to retirement. He mounted the four-wheeler, then rode it backwards off the ramp.

"You get my message?" Kate asked.

"No." Danny stopped the four-wheeler. "Dispatch got a report of an illegal campfire on Devil's Nose. Seems fire season gets longer each and every dadgum year. What's going on?" He never quit smiling.

"Mo Yamaguchi. You met her when we were moving cattle out at Blue Creek last year."

"Right." Danny furrowed his brow and pushed his wire glasses up with a freckled finger.

"She's up here somewhere and I got a text from her saying somebody with a gun's chasin' her. Shot her dog. I talked to her for a second and she was panicked, then, I lost her. I don't know if her phone died, or…" The thought planted a lump in Kate's throat and tears in her eyes. She shook her head.

"Holy crap, Kate!"

"And Gus is out here too, some goddamn place. We have to—"

Danny K. interrupted, "Did she say where she was?"

"No. Can't you track her phone or something?" Kate wrapped loose hair around her ears.

"I can't, but the sheriff's department sure can. Did you call them?"

"Yeah, but you know how it is. We're on our own. It'll be dark by the time they get their shit together."

"True. Very true." Danny rubbed his chin. "At least, they can get a location based on where her cellular phone last pinged. Her provider stores that data, but it takes hours to retrieve. Good grief." Danny snatched his olive green cap off the tailgate and pulled it on. "I'll call Dispatch and see what they say about the matter."

"Can you open the gate and let me through? I wanna start looking."

"Hold on." Danny unsnapped a big radio from his belt and brought it to his mouth. "Delores. Come in. I have an emergency situation—over."

Danny and Kate waited a few agonizing moments for a response.

"Go ahead," a woman's voice finally crackled over the tiny speaker.

"I'm on 7N08 about a mile and a half *west* of Forest Creek bridge. I have Kate Callahan here. She received contact from one Maureen Yamaguchi—female, claiming pursuit by a male subject with a firearm in the vicinity of

Forest Creek. Sheriff's department has been notified. Over."

Static. And then, "Stand by. Over." Her grainy voice pierced the air. He slipped the radio back into its holster and looked at Kate.

"Since we don't really know what exactly is going on out there, I can't have you endangering yourself. Who knows what we'd be walking into. It's simply too dangerous. Heck, I don't even have my bulletproof vest yet. Still on back order if you can believe it. Best option is to wait for backup."

"You wait all you want. I'm gonna find my friend and my grandson."

"Kate. Please. If something were to happen to you, they could hold me responsible. And it *would* be my fault."

"And if something happens to Mo or Gus while we're standing here debating, it would be *my* fault. You gonna unlock the gate?"

"I can't jeopardize it. It's too dangerous. We'll wait for the sheriff."

"You wait," Kate snarled and stomped back to her truck, anger swelling. She parked the truck off the road, opened the passenger door, and snatched up her red plaid Filson. With her arms in the warm wool coat, she buttoned it and slipped on a small backpack. In the glove box, she found the Smith & Wesson semi-automatic and shoved it inside her coat pocket. She slammed the door. Marching toward Danny K., Kate's nostrils flared as she chewed her lower lip—refusing to look away.

"Kate. Come on. You're putting me in a very difficult situation."

Kate stopped and stuck her finger in his face. "Mo's in a

difficult situation. Not you." She shook as she moved through the mountain misery and around the gate.

"Kate. I'm serious. You need to stop." He followed her. "I'm *ordering you* to stop."

Kate stomped with Danny K. on her heels.

"Kate, you're disobeying direct orders from a federal officer." He stopped.

Kate sent a high middle finger as she went. "Enjoy retirement, you chickenshit."

"I can arrest you."

Kate stopped. Crossed her arms and turned around. "Listen here, Dudley fucking Do-Right, I can shoot you in the foot if you try. You can retire early and won't look like such a *pussy*."

"Don't say that, Kate. Jeez. We're friends and I'd honestly hate to see you get hurt."

Kate walked away.

"You know the odds of finding her alive?" he yelled. "There's a reason 'Calaveras' means skull."

She knew. Everyone in the county knew what happened when someone went missing in these woods.

Chapter Three

At high noon, August Buller was napping in his hammock. A gentle breeze rocked him like a baby, back and forth, for over an hour of peaceful bliss. When he awoke, he interpreted the sky. Clouds took shape and migrated west. Elephants and whales and hippopotamuses on parade. Without warning, the white mammals morphed into a whimsical Rorschach test. Gus was sick of tests and now that he was legally an adult, he refused to take part in them ever again. He shook his Magic 8 Ball.

"Will I...find gold today?" He stopped shaking the ball and watched the circular window until the triangular answer emerged through the blue liquid.

"Outlook...not so good." Gus nodded. Fine by him. The Magic 8 Ball saved Gus so much time and effort. Every day for the last month, he'd asked the ball to predict whether the day would be a boom or a bust. So far, the ball had been correct. Every time it read *Signs point to yes*, or *It is certain*, or *You may rely on it*, Gus found gold on his Forest

Creek claim. Not enough to buy back the ranch, but enough to keep the dream alive.

Rather than waste time and energy digging, detecting, or panning, he sang, "Fire on the mountain," and rolled out of the hammock onto all fours. The Magic 8 Ball rode the swinging hammock. On his butt, Gus pulled his rubber boots on over filthy socks, then lifted his fanny pack, hanging from a nail on a nearby dogwood, and strapped it around an abundant belly that never failed to cause him to feel bad about being pudgy. Gus went nowhere without his fanny pack.

The bear-proof cooler sat wedged and barricaded with rocks in the creek. Deep enough to keep it cold. The second Gus unlatched the lid, Benny, his brown burro, pricked his twenty-eight-inch ears and brayed from behind the canvas teepee. It was the only thing about the animal Gus did not appreciate. The noise was loud—too loud—and loud noises hovered around him and reverberated between his ears the way a bell does even when it's done ringing. Noise never failed to spook Gus. For the first few years of school, he kept cotton stuffed inside his ears. That was when kids started calling him Short Bus Gus.

Inside the creek cooler were four juice boxes, a half-full bag of Fritos, one pack of hot dogs, a half-eaten stick of salami, a can of Cheez Whiz, a whole slew of Go-Gurt yogurt tubes, and the last package of gummy worms. Warm gummies were too soft and not as chewy and yummy as cold ones. Gus had enough supplies to get through the next few days; then he could go home, hug his mom, and eat at the dinner table like normal people.

Since setting up his claim four months ago, no man or beast had messed with or stolen any of Gus's grub. Camp had turned out better than he had imagined when the idea of spending the summer on Forest Creek first hit him. Danny K. had hauled the teepee on his quad and Benny, who stood tall at 14.2 hands, as stout as any Mammoth jack, hauled the rest.

The teepee had belonged to Gus's dad, but when they lost the buffalo ranch, he shoved it into a storage shed behind their new home in the trailer park. Six months later, someone busted into the shed and stole everything but the heavy canvas and long wooden poles. Gus and Danny K. had the teepee standing and secured near the creek in under two hours. The next day, Gus chopped down a dozen pecker poles and built a small shelter for Benny behind the teepee, because donkeys hate rain.

In his teepee at night, Gus reread the same old books. Edward Abbey's *The Monkey Wrench Gang, The Art of War,* and *Sex for Dummies* by Dr. Ruth Westheimer, and when the urge to draw struck him, he'd use the black end of a burned stick to recreate the walls of the Chauvet Cave. Miss Mo had explained about the prehistoric French cave paintings after Gus shared a portrait he'd drawn of the love of his life, Gloria. By the end of summer, the canvas walls featured running horses, roaring lions, standing bears, jumping fish, and Gloria—smiling because she never smiled.

In the dark, with a good fire going, the charcoal Gloria would come to life. Her big brown eyes would follow him and the animals would flicker on the canvas walls like a vintage film. Sometimes he'd stare at her long silky black hair and a terrible sadness would creep up on him. That sadness usually worked into what Miss Mo assured Gus was a panic attack. It was like being strangled while his heart kicked and bucked and felt like it would explode with each blow. He suffered attacks every day for the first week after Gloria dumped him until Miss Mo prescribed sticking his head or his face, Gus couldn't quite remember which, in ice-cold water or snow. Miss Mo treated him like an adult and printed out copies of two separate clinical trials proving cold therapy had helped patients suffering from PTSD and panic attacks.

Not an hour after that session with Miss Mo, a panic attack struck. Gus tried to remain calm as he asked his mom to disregard the way home and drive him to Wilson Lake as quickly as possible. When she asked why, Gus replied, "Mom, it…is an emergency." She almost drove the speed limit, but braked too much around the curves. One mile up the road seemed to take forever. "Please hurry, Mom." Gus rolled down the window. Even stuck his head out to keep from coming apart.

When Mom stopped the car next to Wilson Lake, which was more of a big pond than a lake, Gus fled. His short legs pumping with his arms. He hadn't noticed the thin sheet of glassy ice at the far end until he reached the water. As Miss Mo had instructed, he tried to submerge only his head and face, but the shore was too gradual. Before his heart could explode, Gus trotted out waist-deep into Wilson Lake, pinched his nose, and sunk. The shock drowned the panic attack. Although he'd given his mom a good scare, he couldn't wait to share the good news with Miss Mo.

Gus sucked on the tiny straw in the juice box as Benny bobbed his head and hopped his way over with hobbled front legs. Up and down hee-hawing as he moved forward. Determined to get there before the juice box emptied.

"Almost gone…buddy." He teased, but always left a few swallows for Benny. Whiskers tickled Gus's cheek as the burro nosed the juice. "Okay." Gus pulled out the straw and held the box to Benny's lips. The burro slurped as Gus squeezed. Juice drained from the little hole until it was gone.

"Delores. Come in. I have an emergency situation, over." The garbled voice came over the walkie talkie, but Gus knew Danny K.'s voice.

Rubber boots slapped at his knees as he ran to his teepee. He threw back the canvas flap and hurried inside.

"Go ahead," her voice chirped as Gus grabbed the radio off a log stump next to his bedroll and listened.

"I'm on 7N08 about a mile and a half *west* of Forest Creek bridge. I have Kate Callahan here. She received contact from one Maureen Yamaguchi—female, claiming pursuit by a male subject with a firearm in the vicinity of Forest Creek. Sheriff's department has been notified. Over." Ranger Danny K. said.

Gus closed his eyes. His heart punched him from inside. Danny K. was his good friend and now his partner. If it weren't for him, Gus would never have been able to stake his claim. Danny K. took care of all the red tape and paperwork.

"Stand by. Over." Her voice was captivating.

Gus squeezed the radio and his eyes. Rubbed his forehead. Kate Callahan was his grandma and Maureen Yamaguchi was his therapist, and he loved them both. *Shit.*

"Nobody...better...not...hurt Miss Mo." The words clung to his fear. He pressed the talk button on his radio. "Nobody hurt them!" He wanted to cuss out loud, but in his head was easier. *Fuck!* He'd never said that bad of a word out loud, and he never would. He grabbed his backpack, shoved the radio inside, and hurried for the exit, but wasn't clear where to go. Save Miss Mo or protect Grammy Kate?

In his haste, he kicked a rock away from the smoldering fire pit in the middle of the teepee. Gus reached down and replaced the rock. He grabbed a hunk of firewood when he remembered he had to hurry.

"Forget...it." His words were going to glitch more and more like when the Wi-Fi was no good. It happened whenever Gus was afraid or nervous and there wasn't a thing he could do about it. The more he tried, the worse it got. The words. In his head, they were as clear and flowed as easy as creek water. But somewhere in the back of his throat the words hit a snag, a sandbar behind his tongue, and no matter how hard he fought, his speech floundered.

He secured the teepee with tie straps and grabbed the Magic 8 Ball off the hammock, his coat from a broken branch, and the package of gummy worms and Cheez Whiz from the creek. Water and granola bars were still in his pack from yesterday.

Leaving his gold pan, metal detector, a variety of hammers, and two shovels lying around made him nervous. He should put them in the teepee, but he had to prioritize. "Bye...Ben." He waved goodbye to the burro standing in the shade.

Gus worked his way across the creek. A miserable mosquito pierced his cheek and he smacked it hard. Blood on his hand meant he'd killed one of the last rotten mosquitos of the season. Next it would be the ticks sucking his blood. Ticks and mosquitos were way worse than bears or mountain lions.

After plodding three miles, hunger panged. Gus remembered the granola bar in his backpack, but he'd have to wait. That way he wasn't eating as soon as he got hungry. He wanted to lose weight after Gloria broke up with him and Miss Mo had suggested he practice using willpower.

She explained how everyone has willpower, but some people have strong willpower and some people have weak willpower. Gus knew his was weak and he had to strengthen it.

Willpower lasted about ten minutes. Gus stopped, sat on a rock, took off his backpack, and dug out the granola bar. The firm chocolate tasted great. He drank from a hose connected to a water bladder inside his pack, then tucked the granola wrapper inside his pants pocket. He was no litter bug.

Clouds churned and threatened rain as Gus approached the bridge. Movement caught his attention. His heart sped up when Grammy Kate approached the bridge.

"Gus." She sounded relieved. "Thank God."

Gus ran to her like a tired and hungry man, because he was. She held open her arms and hugged him tight. Hugging her was better than eating. Gus's birth mom was Grammy Kate's daughter, Emma Lee, but she was too young and had to give Gus up for adoption. After sixteen years, Grammy Kate had found him. He didn't know how, but it didn't matter. He was grateful to have a grandma and loved her a lot.

"Where you goin'?" she asked.

"I was…looking…for you." He had to keep Grammy Kate safe from the bad guys who were after Miss Mo.

"Me? How'd you know I was here?"

"I heard it…on the radio…Danny K. gave me." Gus stepped back from Grammy Kate, remembering about the emergency. "He said you were here…and…there is an emergency."

"Yes, hon. You got that little SOS transmitter thing I bought you?"

"I lost it…in the creek."

LISA MICHELLE

"Shit. It's Miss Mo. Someone's trying to hurt her and—"

"I saw…Miss Mo."

"You *did?* When?"

"A long time ago."

"What do you mean? When?"

"Not today. A while…back." Gus tried his best to recall when exactly he saw her. "Over there. She…parked…her bike." Gus pointed up the hill from the bridge.

"Gus, Mo might be hurt. It's possible that something bad happened. I got a text from her. She said a man shot Walter and was chasing her. I only talked to her for a second, but she sure sounded scared."

"Shot *Walter?*" Why shoot an innocent dog? Before he knew it, his hands had turned to fists. Walter was always at Miss Mo's office when Gus had his weekly visits. He loved that dog. His ears were so soft and he always helped settle Gus's nerves when he shared about things that made him feel bad. Instead of crying, Gus would rub Walter's ears. He was a nice dog who didn't need to be shot.

"That man is…a bad guy."

"Yes, Gus. And I'd like you to go to my house. Stay with Ed and the boys. It's not safe right now."

Grammy Kate was the one who was not safe. She should go home. "Why…are you…here?" Gus asked.

"Because Mo's my friend. And I have to do whatever I can to help her."

"Miss Mo is…my friend too. Maybe…my *best* friend. You…should go home…and let me…find her."

"No. No way you're staying out here by yourself!"

"You…are not…the boss of me."

"What?" Grammy Kate crossed her arms. "Okay, fine. But still. No. Not safe."

36

"I will...go home...with you. You can...take me. Right now! Let's go!" Gus's lips extended in an exaggerated pout. He crossed his arms too, stood his ground, and lowered his chin. Only his eyes moved up to Grammy Kate. He raised his brow and waited. "It's not...safe here."

Chapter Four

Kate and Gus stood on the wooden bridge, eyeing each other as the creek babbled beneath them. Kate looked away first—up at the swaying treetops. She knew Gus was nineteen and though he had certain disabilities, he was an adult and not prone to heeding her advice. Being his grandmother for only the last four years did not allow her to set his speed and direction. After all, she was to blame for his adoption. She was the one who'd left him at the church an hour after her teenage daughter delivered him. What kind of grandmother does that? Although wonderful and loving parents raised a brilliant young man, Kate would live with the guilt and regret of giving Gus up for the rest of her life.

"I love you, Gus." Kate looked at the man who looked like a boy, his glasses sitting crooked on his chubby face. "I'm only trying to keep you safe."

"I...I know...but I...been in search...and rescue...for two years. I had to pass...a test. Walk eight...miles...in three hours...with twenty pounds...in my backpack. I did ten…miles…in three hours…with forty pounds. I know… these woods better than you." The side of his mouth smiled. "We camped…here…since I was…a kid."

He was right. Gus knew these woods and Kate had once again judged him unfairly. She knew his parents had taught him to camp and fish and be capable in the outdoors. "I can't believe you've been camped out here all summer."

Gus scanned the sky as if it perplexed him. He held up four filthy fingers. "Four months."

If Gus had been self-sufficient for four months alone in these woods playing gold miner, he would be a benefit to finding Mo, and no way Kate would leave him alone in the wilderness with a gunman on the loose. No way. She crossed her arms. "Soon as we get back, you're taking a damn shower, Mountain Man."

"Okay." Gus smiled and hugged her.

"And I'll cut your hair. If you want," she added.

"Okay."

"I love you." She kissed the top of his head, then tousled his stringy hair. It smelled like sour milk and wood smoke.

"I love you too." His words didn't stick for once. He never hesitated to show his true feelings or affection for Kate, or anyone else. It warmed and amazed her to think someone this good and kind could have sprung from someone as horrible as his biological father. Thanks to Mo, Kate had learned how to use her guilt to build a loving relationship with Gus.

"Want…to see…where Miss Mo…parked her bike… last time…I saw her…here?"

"Yes. Yes."

"Up here." Gus turned back and scampered across the bridge to the north. Kate followed. He veered west, up a slope. Before starting into the trees, there it stood. Mo's mountain bike parked behind a boulder, waiting for her like a trusty steed.

"Okay." Kate unzipped the panniers that hung over the rear tire.

"What…are you looking for?" Gus asked.

"I have no idea." Kate pulled out an empty liter of aloe juice and a collapsible dog bowl. She unzipped the opposite side and found a tire repair kit, a pair of flip-flops, and the tiny pink canister of pepper spray Kate had given her last year. She stuffed the canister into her pocket and looked at the creek. Turned her head left then right. "Up or down?" She cupped her icy hands alongside her mouth and yelled as loud as she could. "Mo!"

Gus pressed his hands over his ears and closed his eyes. "Stop."

Kate had forgotten his sensitivity to loud noises. "Oh no." She rushed to him and held his head. "I'm so sorry. I forgot."

Gus looked down. Took his hands off his ears and studied the ground. He took a step forward. Slowly, he moved as if he were tracking something. At the creek, he stopped and looked over at Kate.

"What?" She asked.

"This way," he pointed, "she followed…the creek. Upstream."

Kate scanned the ground for footprints, dog shit, anything. "I don't see it. You sure?" she asked.

"Yes…I'm sure."

"Okay." She patted him on the back as he turned to go. Kate didn't understand how Gus knew the way, but she trusted him and followed.

They zigzagged along the creek shore over dried rocks that on an average year would still be underwater. The warm arms of the sun had pulled away and turned the autumn sky a dirty gray.

"Maybe...she got a...ride home." Gus had always talked a lot, but he hadn't been quiet once since tracking Mo.

"I doubt it. There's no roads around here." Kate caught herself getting irritated for no good reason other than her best friend had gone missing.

"Yes...there are. If...she...could get there. You...have to...think positive. Don't...be negative."

"Okay, sure. She got lucky and found a road where there just happened to be some nice person driving by who stopped and gave her a ride home. Uh-huh."

Kate fought the urge to scream out for Mo again, if nothing else, to silence Gus for a few moments, but held back. A barricade of boulders and rock mixed with fallen trees had washed down the canyon and wedged themselves in a tangled mess that forced the two uphill and around.

"How come Miss Mo...doesn't live with you anymore?" Gus climbed over a downed cedar.

"I don't know. She just needed her space," Kate lied and straddled the log. Mo moved out soon after Kate had mentioned that kids at the Calaveras County Frog Jump had teased the twins about having two moms. Kate had listened as Patrick explained to the older girl that his mom was in heaven and that he and his brother lived with Grammy and Mo Mo. Ed told her that more than a few people had assumed two women living together must be gay. Kate never cared what anyone thought of her, but hated seeing the boys being harassed. She never asked or wanted Mo to move out, but didn't try to stop her when she did.

42

"But Miss Mo was…your best friend…right?"

"Is. She *is* my best friend." *And my only friend.* Kate followed Gus around the demolition of trees.

"I think…it would be…cool…to live…with your best friend."

"It was." Guilt gnawed at her. Mo rented a house with an office near town. They swore they'd visit every week, continue having Sunday dinners, take the twins on walks. But after only a month it became more and more of an effort and after two months it didn't happen.

Kate missed Mo at dawn. It seemed the only thing they had in common was being early risers. They'd sit, drink coffee, and debate everything from politics to the deeper meaning of the weird dreams they'd had the night before. There were never two more opposite best friends. Mo, well educated, tall, and thin and Kate, a college dropout, short, and stout.

"You believe…in God?" Branches cracked as Gus bull-dozed his way through manzanita brush thick and sticky as any jungle.

"Not the God you learned about in church every Sunday." Kate followed, puffing, sweating, and focused on searching for any sign of Mo.

"What about…Jesus? You know…he died for…us."

"My faith has nothing to do with religion." Kate said, out of breath. She had no problem putting in a hard day's work, but had little use for aerobic type exercise. Her heart pummeled in her chest. She unbuttoned her wool coat, flapping it like wings. Forcing cool air inside.

"Do you like…hot dogs…or hamburgers better?" Gus stopped and waited.

"Hamburgers," Kate huffed, but could not have cared less. Food never impressed her. She had always been an easy keeper and ate whatever was available. Her head throbbed.

"I...love hot dogs." Gus hiked uphill and looked down at Kate. "There...is a...deer trail." He waited again for Kate to catch up. Her quads were on fire as she climbed and coughed. A stabbing pain flared up in her right foot from where a cow had stepped on it last week. She'd thought it had healed and forgotten all about it until now.

"You...okay?" he asked as Kate struggled, but she didn't dare complain or whine when Mo could have a bullet in her.

Kate stopped, coughed more, and caught her breath. "We're burnin' daylight." She smiled and patted Gus on the back.

"I got some...hot dogs...at camp."

"Cover your ears."

Gus slapped his hands over his ears.

"Mo!" Kate screamed. They stopped and looked around. Kate pressed her index finger to her lips, signaling Gus to be quiet.

Little by little, he moved his hands off his ears. Keeping them only inches away from his head in case of a second uproar.

"Let's just listen awhile, okay? I can't hear if Mo calls for help if you're talking all the time."

Gus nodded, lowered his hands, and walked.

Pine needles and leaves crunched under every step until the stench stopped them both in their tracks.

"What the hell is that?" Kate asked.

"Something...is dead." Gus turned around, pinching his nose.

"I know, but what?" Kate didn't mean to sound so

sarcastic. It was the thought of death coming to a head. Her eyes scoured the surrounding woods.

Gus moved forward and stepped off the barely-there game trail. Kate watched him. "What are you doing?" He didn't answer. Just looked at the ground. "Gus?" He grabbed a small stick and bent over, inspecting and poking something with the stick. "Gus?" He stayed hunched over, eyes to the ground, stepping slowly.

"Uh-oh." Gus stopped and Kate hurried toward him.

"What?" she insisted.

Gus shot a worried look at Kate.

Kate looked down at the carcass. A doe. Her eye open and glassy. Exposed teeth wide above a long blue tongue that hung from her open mouth—holding in one last silent cry for help. Her stomach and half her rib cage—gone. Leaves and dirt and debris covered the lower part of the carnage. Kate did her best not to think of Mo, but visions of her slender body lying bloody and broken on the cold ground drove Kate to look away. She rubbed her face with her palms. "Let's go, Gus."

Gus knelt next to the doe's head and moved the hair on the back of her neck with his stick. Two puncture marks confirmed it.

"Mountain lion…killed her."

Kate knew a lion kill when she saw one. And it seemed Gus did too. "Yep…lets go." Gus stood still staring at the doe. He slapped his stick at a fat tick burrowed into the doe's shoulder. "Watch out…for ticks," Gus said, and walked away.

Kate wondered if ticks were digging into Mo. "I hate ticks." Kate turned away from the kill.

Once they gained elevation, the manzanita cleared and a trail became obvious. The going got easier as the terrain gradually leveled and trees eventually thinned. The creek came back into view. Below them, the forest blazed with a fire that didn't consume it. Autumn trees turned to torches of red and orange. Forest Creek snaked its way through sheer granite walls, high and perfect as if someone had built them.

"There's no way we're getting down there," Kate said. "And Mo would never have come this way."

"She would…if…she…was running," Gus said and swiped sweaty bangs off his glasses.

"Plug your ears." Kate waited until Gus covered his ears. She took the deepest breath she could.

"MAUREEEEEN!" She looked up and down, to the creek below and listened. "Mooooo!" A tragic silence squelched what little hope she had left.

"This is stupid," Kate said, and Gus dropped his arms away from his ears and down to his sides. "She could be dying in that brush right there," Kate pointed to a patch a few yards below, "and we'd never know it. We'd walk right by her."

Kate couldn't recall a time she didn't appreciate being in these woods. Nature had always worked wonders on her soul. Ancient trees whispered mysterious secrets to the wind. Stoic mountains stood against eons of violent blizzards. Motley rocks placed like decorative sculptures. Sparrows and juncos chirped while ravens argued and all of it made perfect sense. Offered a belief that the world was right, people were wrong. Now all Kate could see in the forest she loved was the ugly truth. An alluring facade that hid death and destruction.

How many men and women had gone missing in these woods? Kate had lost track over the three decades in Calaveras County. How many missing weren't even accounted for in the sheriff's missing persons file? Once they disappeared, the wilderness seemed to have consumed them. Not a single one found alive. Not the young mother discovered stuffed into a fifty-five-gallon steel drum. Not the guy wrapped in orange plastic fencing and shot by his mother in their marijuana garden. And not the dozens who "accidentally" overdosed and wandered off into the woods after not paying their dealer for their last fix.

The heartbreak, like the memorial crosses, went on for miles along the back roads. All because of drugs. When you dug deep enough, most crime came back around to drugs. Kate shivered and wondered how many addicts Mo had helped get clean. Get their lives together and their children back. How many had she saved? Would they show up in the cold dark to return the favor? Not likely, Kate thought.

Gus sat on a rock and slipped off his backpack. "She asked me to go with her," Kate confessed, sitting down next to him, "but I had to split firewood." She slipped out of her backpack. "Bet Mo invited me at least a dozen times to go hiking, or fishing, or camping. There was always somethin' more important. Always next time." Tears filled her eyes. Now, there might not be a next time. Kate foraged for a bottle of water in her backpack. "You got water?"

"Yes." Gus smiled. "And...gummies." He held up his package of gummy worms. "Did you know...that real worms...don't have bones...but gummy worms are... made...out of gelatin...which is made...from bones...so gummy worms...have more bones...than real worms."

Kate grinned, then laughed. "How'd you get so smart?"

"Reading...and YouTube. And...my mom...and dad."

Kate had met Gus's adoptive parents and knew they'd likely done a better job raising him than she could have. Yet she wished she had found the strength to find him sooner. "You still watch Jeopardy every night?" she asked.

"No TV…at camp."

"I know. I meant—never mind." Kate looked at her watch. "Four twenty."

Gus smirked, "Four twenty."

"Why's that funny?"

"I…don't know." Gus shrugged.

"Oh *yes* you do. What?"

"Kids…smoke weed…at four-twenty. After school." Gus laughed. "Four-twenty…means you like weed."

"You smoke that shit?" Kate asked.

"My friends do." Gus looked offended. "I'm…not stupid. Weed…affects…your brain. My brain…has enough…problems."

"You're brighter than a lot of well-educated idiots I know." Kate scrutinized the land as far as she could see, hoping for a hint of odd color or movement that would lead to Mo. Days were growing noticeably shorter this time of year. "Well…we either turn around now and hope we make it back before it's too dark, or we keep going." Kate didn't care for either option. "Shit." She opened her water bottle and sipped. Her throat burned as she swallowed.

"Today…is the…equinox." Gus offered Kate some of his gummy worms.

"No thanks." Kate slid her water bottle into the mesh side pocket of her backpack and swung it on. "You have a headlamp?" she asked, stuffing her icy hands into her coat pockets, wishing she'd brought gloves.

"Yes," Gus said with a bright green worm hanging from his mouth. "What should…we do?"

"I don't know." Kate leaned forward and buried her head in her hands—wanting to cry, but coughing instead.

"We have to find her. No matter how hard or uncomfortable it gets." Kate looked up, beat her fists against the rock and stomped her feet like a child throwing a tantrum. "Fuck."

With Gus watching, she settled down and wiped her eyes. Wind kicked down dead leaves. Gus's long hair whipped at his face. He looked up, so did Kate. Ashen clouds smothered the sky.

Chapter Five

It smelled like rain. Gus rubbed Kate's back while they sat on the rock.

"Miss Mo will be okay." His words didn't flutter, and he hoped that meant he was right. If anyone hurt her, he would have to kick butt. "I will save her...because she... saved me," Gus said with a renewed enthusiasm. Miss Mo had saved him. When Gloria dumped him, Gus not only thought he would die, he preferred it. The pain became unbearable. Worse than when a rambunctious hunter shot his pet buffalo Eeyore.

Gus couldn't sleep. He couldn't eat, even when he was hungry. Ruminating on the perfect life he and Gloria had planned in San Francisco took up most of the day and all the night. She planned to leave the Mi-Wuk reservation and help Gus sell his art in Golden Gate Park. Together they'd ride bikes on paved roads, Gloria's long black hair flapping behind her like a cape. They'd watch movies in a theater, something neither of them had done before.

The last official therapy session Gus had with Miss Mo

was months ago, when she explained how having new goals would help to forget his old ones. The new goal became to buy back the buffalo ranch the bank had stolen. Mom could move back home where she belonged and get out of Dunrovin Mobile Home Park. That place was a dump and Gus hated it. Living there only made him sad and that upset his mom. Spending the summer camped on his mining claim worked perfectly. Gus stayed busy learning to discover gold and by the second month on Forest Creek, thoughts of Gloria stopped stabbing at him. For that, he loved Miss Mo and would never let anything bad happen to her.

Grammy Kate stood and unkinked her back. "Let's go." She adjusted her pack and took off back downhill the way they'd come. Gus followed.

"Grammy Kate?"

"Yeah?"

"Is Mr. Ed…your boyfriend?"

"I don't know. Maybe."

"Do you love…him?"

"Hey! Have you ever played that game where the first person who talks loses?"

"I never…heard of it."

"We're starting now. First person to speak loses. Go."

It took all his willpower not to talk. He thought of roasting hot dogs over a campfire in his teepee. He wished he'd brought the half bag of Fritos.

By five o'clock, they'd reached the creek. The temperature dropped with the sun and Gus pulled his zipper up as high as it would go. It seemed like hours since he'd spoken, but couldn't be since it wasn't night yet.

"This…is a dumb…game," Gus said.

Kate turned. "I win." She watched him dig in his backpack. He found a red Buffalo Bills beanie and put it on. Not that he liked the Buffalo Bills or football even. It was the big blue buffalo emblem sewn on the front of the beanie that he liked.

"I'm starving," Gus groaned.

"I know. Me too, but we need to get moving. It's getting dark and I think it's gonna rain."

"I...have to pee." Gus dropped his backpack on the sand.

"Me too." Kate walked ahead, then disappeared into the trees.

Gus stood behind a big rock and unzipped his pants. He'd waited too long and if he didn't hurry, he might wet himself. He drew a line back and forth in the sand. When he finished, he dipped his hands in the creek and rinsed them. A dead fish floated upside down near the shore. Gus looked around. Another fish floated downstream. Gus wondered what would have killed the fish and not eaten them.

"Come on," Kate shouted from somewhere ahead.

"Hold on." Gus pulled the Cheez Whiz from his backpack, then zipped it fast, and swung it on as he trotted to catch up with Grammy Kate.

They hiked single file, Gus following along the zigzagging tracks they'd made earlier, around and up over rocks like an obstacle course on the dry portion of the creek bed. Gus sprayed Cheez Whiz in his mouth and worked his tongue around until he'd swallowed it all. Chewing Cheez Whiz didn't work very well unless you had crackers.

"Grammy Kate?"

"Yeah?"

"Do you...think about...my real mom?"

"All the time." Kate looked back at Gus for a moment, but kept moving.

"I think...of her...all the time...too. I wish...I knew her."

"I know, hon. It's beyond complicated. You could come stay with us. Spend time with your little brothers."

Gus stopped. The thought of staying the night with Grammy Kate and being a big brother had never occurred to him. "I would...love that!"

"There's plenty room. You can't camp in the winter. Come stay." She said it like a question that needed an answer.

"I will do it!" Gus bounced up and down on his toes and wished they could go there now. "You can tell me...about my father." Gus knew she had a good reason for refusing to talk about his biological father. But he had faith, like an innocent pup who'd never been beaten, that people were mostly good, and that included his biological father.

Kate stopped, but she didn't look back at him. "I hated your dad. Plain and simple. Sorry, but that's the truth."

"You mean...my father. He's...not my dad."

"Right. Well, I don't want to say bad things about him. No good will come of it." She walked faster than before and for once Gus had trouble keeping up. Especially while trying to eat Cheez Whiz.

Dark spots appeared on dry rocks and speckled them like drab Easter eggs. Thunder rumbled and rolled through the canyon. Gus filled his mouth with the last of the Cheez Whiz and shoved the empty can in his coat pocket.

Daylight had turned gritty with the help of rain by the time they reached the bridge. "Shit," Grammy Kate mumbled, but Gus heard it. He wished she wouldn't cuss so much. "I thought we'd have some goddamn help up here by now. Sheriff was notified hours ago. They should have got a hold of Search and Rescue. Something for Christ's sake!"

Kate slammed her hands on her hips and looked madder than Gus had ever seen her. His stomach knotted.

"Maybe...they don't...want to get wet." He wasn't joking.

"Probably right. Bunch a chicken shits." She turned in slow circles on the bridge.

"I'm going...back to camp." Gus took off his wet glasses and put them in his jacket pocket. "Benny...will be... hungry." He wiped his face with the back of his sleeve and pulled his hood over his hat.

"Who's Benny?"

"My burro."

"How far is your camp?"

"Far." Gus hugged Grammy Kate. "I will...keep looking. You...go home." Gus turned away and crossed the bridge, hoping she would go home where she'd be safe.

"Gus!" She ran towards him. "I—can't leave you...out here all alone. I—" Now her words were sticking. "No one will show up until tomorrow. Am I supposed to just go home, take a shower, eat dinner while my best friend is..." Grammy Kate grabbed her mouth. Tears ran down her cheeks.

Gus had never seen her cry and it scared him. He was taking too much time to decide. He never knew why he'd been so good at making bad decisions until it was too late. After rubbing his cold ears, he decided. "You cannot...help. It's...dark! And...raining...for Christ's sake! Shit." Gus liked the way his borrowed words sounded. *Serious—like a real badass.* "Go...home! I got this!" He knew it was the right decision, but he didn't mean it.

He wanted her with him. Spending time with his real grandmother and having someone to talk to was what normal people did. They could talk about all kinds of things. Get to know each other better. And most of all, maybe they could discuss his birth mother. More than anything, Gus wanted to know about his biological father, especially since Gus's dad, the man who'd loved and raised him, had died of coronavirus six months ago. Maybe hanging out together, drinking hot cocoa in his teepee would help her understand how important the truth was to him.

Grammy Kate crossed her arms as Gus slipped off his backpack. He dug around inside until he found his head lamp and worked it over his hood. He clicked the light on and Grammy Kate blocked her eyes with her hand. "Jeez, Gus."

"Sorry." He bent over and aimed his light at something on the ground.

"What?"

"Thought so." Gus looked up at her. "It's lion poop."

"Fucking great."

"You cuss…too much." Gus clomped away toward camp with her nipping at his heels.

Grammy Kate strapped her headlamp on and coughed.

"You are getting…sick," Gus said, "like…my dad."

"I'm fine." She coughed, loosening the headlamp's adjustable elastic strap.

"Did you…get your vaccine?"

Grammy Kate nodded. "Yesterday. Some people have a reaction to the shot. Guess I'm one of 'em."

"I don't want…you to die." Gus couldn't imagine losing Grammy Kate too. Especially since they'd only just found each other a few years ago.

"I'm too damn ornery to die. How much farther?"

"One…mile." Gus didn't mind being cold and wet. It

wasn't fun, but life wasn't meant to be fun, especially when you had goals.

"You have a tent, right?"

"No. A teepee…and…dry firewood. We can cook hotdogs."

"You got coffee?"

"No. Makes…me jittery. I…have hot cocoa."

"Sounds good. How do you—" The cracking of branches silenced and stopped her. Gus heard it too and froze. They turned, looking toward the brush to the right, and waited for something to confirm their concern, turning to fear. Silence buzzed in Gus's head for far too long. He jerked out the Glock from his fanny pack and held his breath for whatever came next.

A single twig snapped as sharp as an ax banging rock. Gus ripped his headlamp off, bent over, and shined it into a dark opening between thick manzanita. The beam sliced and hunted against the tangled brush. Green glowing eyes rose through drops of rain and Gus almost screamed.

Chapter Six

Kate reached inside her coat and pulled out the .38. Held her finger on the cold trigger. A million thoughts banged around inside her head.

It could be the guy. The guy with the gun.

We should run. But what if it's Mo and she's hurt and can't call out to us?

We have to find out. We have to wait. Shit. What if it is a mountain lion? She doubted her pistol would stop a mountain lion on the attack.

At what point do I make noise? Act bat-shit crazy and try to appear larger than I am?

The tension twisted her tighter and tighter and she let go a scream that started with a growl and ended with a bloodcurdling howl. Gus dropped his headlamp and gun. He covered his ears.

After the screaming, the sound of rain shredded the silence. Gus retrieved his gun and headlamp, steadying them on the bushes with both hands.

"You got a gun?" Kate asked. "Why do you have a

gun?" Her eyes roaming back and forth from Gus to the bushes.

"Why…do you?" He stayed focused on whatever hid in that brush.

A whimper came from somewhere. Kate was fairly sure mountain lions didn't whimper but grabbed a stick and aimed her gun just in case. She knelt and tipped her head-lamp down toward the sound. Gus did the same. With both lights and guns pointed at the brush, blond hair stood out. Mo wasn't blond, but mountain lions were.

"Shit." Kate stepped back and pulled Gus with her. The animal sat up and gave another whimper.

"Holy shit!"

"Holy…shit!" Gus mimicked and tucked his gun back into his fanny pack, then unbuckled and set it on the ground. He strapped his headlamp on his head and shook his backpack off.

"Walter! Sweetheart. Oh, thank God. Come here boy. Come." Kate knelt and called as Gus flopped onto his belly in the mud and wiggled his torso into the manzanita.

"Dogs…can't talk, Grammy. They…don't understand… English," Gus informed her as he army crawled deeper into the brush.

Kate shined her light on Walter. His big brown eyes bulging with fright. Blood glazed his ear and the top of his head. Half of his face crusted with dirt and blood.

"It's his ear. It's split in half." Kate squinted and leaned forward for a closer look. "Come here Walter boy." He didn't move forward, but he didn't back away either.

"Hey, boy." Gus reached for him. "It's…okay, buddy." Gus wrapped his arms around Walter and backed out of the brush on his knees. "You…know me…I'm a good… guy."

When they emerged, Gus set Walter down. The dog was damp and shivering, but the thick manzanita had sheltered him from the soaking storm. Gus kissed the top of Walter's nose. "You're...okay."

When Walter licked Gus's cheek, Kate slapped her hand over her mouth, not knowing whether to laugh or to cry. Hope resurrected her some as she pulled off her headlamp, using the light and her hands to inspect Walter's injured ear. "Calf ears bleed a lot when you notch 'em." She searched the dog from head to toe, moving his fur, lifting and looking under each leg. She felt his ribs and his chest. "You lucked out, Walter." Kate turned to Gus. "I think the shooter is one shitty shot and the bullet caught Wally's ear. There ain't another mark on him. He's fine."

"God...was watching...over him." Gus nodded and smiled. "Yep."

"Hope he's watching over Mo. She could be nearby! Get your radio and see if you can reach someone."

"Ranger Dan?" Gus asked like he didn't understand.

"Yes. Call him. Tell him where we are and that we found Walter. Tell him to get his ass up here and help."

"Okay. I won't...say a-s-s." Gus walked on his knees and reached his backpack, unzipped it, and dug around inside with the speed and agility of a sloth.

"Poor Wally was just scared shitless by the gunfire and he ran off." She hung her backpack on a branch and grabbed the water bottle from the side pocket, then knelt next to Walter. She twisted off the cap and poured water into her cupped hand.

"Get a drink." He smelled it and turned away. "Okay." Kate took a drink from the bottle, then drizzled the rest over Walter's ear and face to wash away some of the blood and muck. Walter shook his head and Kate stuffed the empty bottle back in her pack.

Gus found the radio and held it up like he'd won a trophy.

"Good, Gus." Kate watched him while he fumbled with the knobs. Finally, he pressed the side and put it to his mouth with both hands.

"Hello? Ranger Dan…this…is Gus. Over." Gus kept the radio at his mouth while he waited. And waited.

Kate rubbed Walter and tried her best to be patient while Gus fooled with a knob atop the radio.

"Ranger Dan…Hello? We need…help…please." Gus leaned forward with the radio.

"That dickhead's probably takin' a bubble bath and left his radio in his truck. That…" Kate shook her head and, per Gus's request, suppressed the urge to cuss Danny K. even more.

"Hello! Anyone." Gus's pleas rose several octaves.

She couldn't help but wish Mo had carried a gun. At least with a firearm, she'd have half a chance. Although Mo was fit, and if she had to, she might outrun a man with a gun, she most definitely would not outrun a mountain lion. A gun would scare off most predators.

The terrible nightmare that they were scouting a corpse came to mind without warning. She shoved the image of Mo's bloody and torn carcass away. Mo would say to stop allowing your thoughts to control you—control your thoughts. Kate had heard it a thousand times before but wished she could hear it now. Now the words were more than simply advice. They were vital.

Gus lowered the radio in defeat. "Wish we could… get rid…of all the bad guys." He smiled, and something about it eradicated Kate's despair.

"I love you, Gus."

"I love you…too…Grammy." Gus lifted the radio once more to his lips. "Ranger…!" He paused, "Come…in… please!"

Walter smelled like a wet dog, but Kate hugged him anyhow and his wagging tail proved he liked it.

"The radio…is dead." Gus said, removing the back of the walkie talkie. He fiddled with the batteries. "I have… new batteries…at camp." Gus replaced the batteries and the cover. With his fingertips, he petted Walter.

"Okay. Let's see if Wally here feels like walkin'." Kate stood, stretched her back, then brushed clumps of mud off her knees.

"I will…cook you…a…hot dog, okay buddy?" Gus looked at Walter as if he was waiting for an answer.

"Dogs don't speak English. Remember?" Kate grinned and coughed while she laughed.

"I forget…sometimes."

"Me too. Walter might not speak English, but he damn sure understands."

"Yeah." Gus buckled his fanny pack, then lifted his backpack off the branch. "Let's go." Gus walked backwards slapping his thighs. "Walter."

Walter wagged his tail and pranced as he followed Gus like nothing bad had happened. Too bad people aren't as resilient, Kate thought. Dread swooped down with a vengeance and attacked from out of nowhere. Mo was out there in the dark forest, cold and wet. Maybe lost. Maybe clinging to life. Maybe not. The familiar dread mutated and erupted into a queasiness as Kate trudged along.

The rain stopped but had soaked the forest. Fluorescent yellow pollen ringed puddles while heavy drops gathered on boughs and pummeled down on Kate.

"Walter…is like Walter…White." Gus said looking down at the dog as he walked ahead.

"Who?" Kate asked.

"Walter White. From…*Breaking Bad*. It's…a series…on TV. And it's…awesome. Walter White is…a good guy… but…he has to…do bad stuff. He…is a badass…just like our…Walter."

"His ear's bleeding again," Kate said.

"Oh…darn." Gus scratched his chin and bent down for a closer look at Walter's injured ear.

"You have tape or super glue at camp?" Kate asked.

Gus thought a minute. "No." He shook his head and walked away. "I can…fix it."

"How much farther?" Fatigue having its way with her. Cold, hungry, tired, and her lower back biting like a son of a bitch. She hadn't thought to grab ibuprofen in her haste to help Mo. Not knowing how best to proceed pissed her off. She'd been pretty good at tracking cattle that had broken through the fence and disappeared into Sierra Pacific land or National Forest. This was something else entirely. This was like getting nowhere fast. She pressed her fingers hard into her forehead.

A helplessness overwhelmed Kate. "Gus!"

He and Walter stopped and looked back.

"How far?"

The expression on Gus's face caught Kate off guard. His brow became heavy between eyes that narrowed in on her. His lips slightly puckered just like his father. That long peculiar moment took her breath away. It was as if Will had suddenly possessed him. Kate's next breath became hard to find with the thought of Will taking up too much room in her head.

She replaced visions of the bastard with Gus and Mo and the twins. Imagined how, when this nightmare was over, they'd gather around the dinner table and celebrate. Mo had taught her the coping mechanism. To think of bad thoughts as if they were a movie in your head. Whenever Will played, she'd switch the channel to something better. Gus, Mo, and the twins were Kate's favorite stations.

"Not far—one...more mile."

"A mile? *Shit.* That's what you said a mile ago."

Gus scrunched his face and raised his brow. "I'm... sorry." He ducked off the trail and stopped in front of a half-dead pine with his hand in his jean pocket. He pulled out a knife and jacked the blade with a flick of his wrist.

"What are you doing?" Kate asked, as Gus stabbed deep into the tree's bleeding sap. Slicing away at the thick clots and gathering them in his palm.

"I'm...gonna fix...Walter's ear." Gus looked down at his cupped hand and cut two more quarter-sized pieces. "Got to...soften it up." He brought both hands to his opened mouth and threw his head back. The sap filled the insides of his cheeks like a chipmunk.

Kate shook her head. "I'm afraid to ask."

Gus signaled for Kate to follow as he walked to the trail. He looked back at her and smiled with bulging cheeks.

Kate couldn't look at Gus and not think of his father. "Sorry for being grumpy back there, hon. I'm just frustrated. It's not your fault."

After about ten minutes of soothing silence, Gus stopped and spit his sap out into his hands. He worked and molded the golden resin until it became a thin square the size of his palms.

"Come here…Walter." Gus said and knelt on both knees. The dog came. "Sit please." Walter sat still while Gus applied, then folded the sap bandage over the injured ear. Gus gently pressed the edges together. "Like…a wonton." He laughed.

"Holy cow." Kate knelt down for a closer look. "You're really something, know that?"

"Yeah." Gus stood looking down at his brilliance. Pride filled his chest and lifted his chin. "You need…a campfire… hot dog."

Kate stood. "We need to find Mo and get her home." Home. Hearing herself made Kate realize how much Mo belonged at home with her and the boys. If given the chance, she'd apologize and do whatever it took to bring her back. Tough shit if people didn't like the fact that two women were living together. Kate wasn't the type to let popular opinion sway her decisions.

"I…will find her…Trust me." Gus turned and walked away. Walter tilted his head and followed.

A dense mist like stubborn smoke hung in the air and encouraged the foreboding that Kate could not shake.

Chapter Seven

Benny brayed before they even stepped foot in camp. How that burro always knew when Gus was nearby baffled him. Must be his big ears, Gus decided.

"I'm coming," he yelled and pushed back his beanie. Wind shoved the clouds and mist, revealing the biggest and brightest moon Gus had ever seen. Forest Creek gleamed under the light as they arrived at camp. "You...can get warm...in my teepee."

"Where are the batteries? For the radio," Grammy Kate asked.

"I will...feed Benny...and...get them."

"I can feed Benny. You get the batteries and get that damn radio workin'."

"Okay. The hay cubes...are...hanging...in the... madrone tree." Gus pointed to a burlap sack hanging from a tree above Benny. He wanted his dinner and stomped his front feet as Grammy Kate approached. She shined her light up and found the rope keeping the feed out of Benny's reach. One end tied to the sack and the other around a smaller tree trunk. Kate pulled the slip knot and lowered the sack. Benny brayed like he hadn't eaten in days as she dumped hay cubes on the ground. Gus stood watching.

"Gus! Get the batteries!"

"Oh. Yeah."

Walter followed Gus into the teepee. The pine sap bandage had held and the dog's split ear had stopped bleeding. "Lay down...and rest, buddy." Gus pointed to his bedroll, and Walter obeyed with an appreciative sigh. "I will...warm you up." He dropped his pack and grabbed two long pinecones from the stack. At the campfire centered in the teepee, he flipped the grate off the rocks and set the pinecones inside. With pieces of split wood and sticks against the sappy cones, he lit them with waterproof stick matches. The sap fizzed, then sizzled and lit the cones on fire.

Kate slipped through the door. "Wow. This is incredible, Gus. It's huge." She walked in and looked up at the small opening at the top.

"I...live here...so—"

"How'd you get this thing out here?"

"Danny K...and his...quad."

"I'm impressed." She dropped her backpack and tossed it next to a stump. "Did you draw all these?" Her finger circled the walls.

"Yes."

"No shit." Her mouth hung open as she took it all in. "God, Gus, this is amazing. You're extremely talented, you know that?"

"Yes."

Kate laughed, covering her mouth as laughter turned to coughing. "You find the batteries?"

Gus looked confused.

"For the walkie talkie." Kate went to the growing fire and held her hands above it."

"I left them...at my mom's trailer." Gus added wood to the fire pit.

Kate's eyes widened. "So...we can't use the walkie talkie?"

Gus shook his head. "Sorry." He hurried to the door flap, opened it, then turned back and raised a finger. "I will...get the hot dogs."

Kate sat on a stump next to the fire and dropped her head into her hands. It seemed she wanted to cry, but Gus thought of it more like a special occasion. Having Grammy Kate in his teepee for the first time excited him. She looked up and coughed until a rumble came from her chest. Her face turned red. Gus knew it wasn't the campfire because the smoke hole at the top of the teepee pulled like it should.

"Grammy Kate, you are...sick." Gus touched her shoulder.

"It's nothing." She took a deep breath.

That was exactly what his dad had said. "It's not...nothing. I'll be back." Gus hurried out of the teepee and down to the creek.

The icy water numbed as he washed his hands and face. He dug out the pack of hot dogs from the cooler and secured the latch. His hand ached with cold as he walked back to the teepee missing his dad and worried sick about Grammy Kate.

Half way to the teepee he heard Grammy Kate talking.

"This is Kate Callahan. Can anyone hear me?"

He hurried inside.

"You there?" She held the walkie talkie and waited.

"You...fixed it?" Gus smiled.

"You had the batteries in backwards, hon," Grammy Kate said kindly.

"Oh." Gus hoped Grammy Kate didn't think he was stupid, but she probably did because putting the batteries in backwards was a pretty dumb thing to do.

"Hello. This is Kate Callahan. I'm with Gus Buller at his camp on Forest Creek and we need help." They waited. "Can anyone hear me?" And waited for a response that didn't come. Kate shook her head and set the walkie talkie down next to her on a stump.

At eight o'clock, Gus tossed a few more pieces of wood on the fire and snatched a long, sharpened roasting stick leaning against the wall. His fingers reminded him of hot dogs as he struggled to open the pack of Oscar Mayer wieners. "I don't...have no buns," he shouted.

"This is Forest Service. Daniel Kilpatrick speaking, hello Kate?"

Kate snatched up the walkie talkie. "Yes! I can hear you. We need help. We found Mo's dog."

"Just to confirm, you *are* with Gus at his gold claim?"

"Yes." She covered her mouth to quiet more coughing.

"Okay. Good. We're dispersing now. Stay where you are. Search and Rescue is coordinating."

"About goddamn time," Grammy Kate said, but not over the radio. "Did you hear we found Mo's dog? Shot!"

Danny K. didn't respond for a long while. "Dead or alive?"

"Alive! The asshole missed. Shot his ear. You might have your people start looking where we found him."

"Where exactly did you locate the dog?"

"On the trail—a mile or so from Gus's claim." Grammy Kate looked to Gus as he shoved the stick through a hot dog. "Gus! Were we south of here?"

He nodded. "Southeast. One...point two-five...miles from here."

"One and a quarter mile southeast of Gus's camp. He was in the long stretch of manzanita brush."

"Okay. Kate. You stay there with Gus. It's much safer for everyone that way. Having you wandering around puts us all at risk. Do you understand?"

"Yeah...stay put," Gus said, giving her a sideways glance while stabbing the stick through another hot dog.

"Okay. Jeez. Just get going please." Grammy Kate might do what Danny K. said. Maybe she finally understood and would let the good guys take care of the bad guys.

Gus held the stick that now held four hotdogs over the fire and began roasting them.

"I'll contact you when we have something. Over," Danny K. said.

"If you find her, be sure to let her know we've got Walter and he's okay."

Grammy Kate set the walkie talkie on the ground next to her.

"You want your...dog well done...or medium?"

"Medium is fine." Grammy Kate coughed and coughed until Gus knew it was not nothing. He stood.

"Here." He handed Grammy the stick loaded up with hot dogs and picked up a leather satchel next to his bedroll and opened it. He felt around until he found what he was looking for and pulled out a plastic bottle of purple liquid. Most of the label had worn away.

"Here, Grammy." Gus tossed the bag on his bedroll and handed Grammy Kate the bottle. "Cough medicine will help."

She traded Gus the medicine for the hot dog stick, then looked at the bottle. "How old's this stuff?"

Gus shrugged his shoulders and lifted his palms. "It's okay...I had some...last night." He didn't think he should tell Grammy Kate that he'd refilled the bottle with the NyQuil that had three big Zs on the label. He started using it after Gloria—when he couldn't sleep, he'd take a few swigs. It helped him make it through the night.

"Jeez." Kate smiled and unscrewed the cap. "You're prepared for everything, aren't you?"

"Boy Scout motto...be prepared."

"You were a Boy Scout?" She tilted her head back and took two big swigs of the grape syrup.

"Yes. Eight years...in a row. A Boy Scout...is trustworthy." Gus looked up and cocked his thumb in the air. "Loyal." His index finger shot out as he counted the qualities. "Helpful, friendly...courteous and kind..." He paused, trying to remember. "Obedient...cheerful...clean." He'd used up almost all his fingers. "Brave!" He smiled. "There are twelve...but I can't remember...the rest."

"That's awesome. You're all those things. You should be very proud of yourself, Gus."

"I am." He smiled.

"I'm proud of you too." She took two more swallows of medicine and put the lid on. "What else don't I know about you?"

"All kinds...of stuff." Gus turned the hot dogs over.

"Like what?"

"Like...maybe I'll tell you if...you tell me something?"

"Sure. Anything."

Gus lifted the stick away from the fire and looked at Grammy Kate as serious as ever. "I want to...know about my father. Not...my dad. My...father."

Grammy Kate didn't answer. She shook her head,

stood, and went to the satchel to put the cough medicine away. "Stop tormenting yourself over what you call your father." She sat on Gus's bedroll next to Walter. "Telling you about him won't do you any good." She coughed.

"That's my choice...not yours." Gus propped the hot dog stick between two campfire rocks and lifted the lid on the ice chest. "I'm an adult." He brought out what was left of a loaf of bread. "You...would...want to...know." The madder he got, the more his words stuck.

"I'm sorry, Gus. Please, just trust me on this issue. The best thing you can do is let it go."

"No way...Never." He sounded like a child and he felt like one too. "It's...my right." Gus used a piece of bread to wrap the hot dog and pull it off the stick. He handed it to his Grammy Kate.

"Thank you."

"I would...tell you...the...truth. If you...asked...me." Gus wrapped another dog around the heel of bread and set it in front of Walter. "Did he...hurt...me? When I was... little. On my head?" Gus needed to understand why his brain worked the way it did and suspected his father may have had something to do with it. His real dad, Mr. Buller, explained how a brain was like a motor and Gus's motor had wires that were crossed or frayed somewhere and kept popping a fuse. If Gus could figure out what had caused the short in his brain, there might be a chance of fixing it.

"Your father never knew about you." Kate bit into her hot dog. "Mmmm. This is great," she said around a mouthful. "Might be the best wiener I've ever had." She chewed, giggled, and coughed.

"Why?" Gus watched Walter eat.

"Why what?"

"Why didn't...he know...about me?" Gus looked at Grammy Kate and tilted his head.

"He died before you were born." She shoved the last of the hot dog in her mouth as Gus glared at her. She was trying hard to deflect without lying.

"How...did he die?" Gus asked.

Chapter Eight

Sidestepping the truth was always easier in the moment. This wasn't the time or the place to explain why she had killed Gus's father. Kate wiped her mouth with the back of her hand as Gus pointed the hot dog stick and offered another.

"You eat. But thanks." His consideration and constant kindness touched her deep inside and she understood that his craving to know about his father wasn't going to stop. Part of her understood he had a right to know who and what his father was as she watched the boy chomp the hot dog from the stick, his cheeks at full capacity as he chewed, then swallowed.

"My mom says…it's not nice…to keep secrets." He took another bite and tears dribbled down his chubby cheeks. Kate hadn't expected tears. It was like a yawn—contagious and stinging her eyes. Guilt overwhelmed her as she considered the last time she'd kept secrets and how they had festered for years until it ruined Emma Lee. If only she'd been honest, maybe things would have worked out. Maybe Em would still be alive and Gus would have his damn truth.

The boy wiped his face with his sleeve. "I already know...what you did." He ate the last hot dog off the stick and glared at Kate. She wished Mo were here to offer her expertise.

"What do you mean?" Kate forced a grin.

"I saw you...on the...news. A long...time ago...when...you were in jail." He put his hand on Kate's shoulder. "I know...about bad stuff. I *can* deal." Gus smiled, bent over, and hugged Kate. "You...killed my grandpa."

Kate's heart bucked and kicked. She couldn't find a single word or a place to start. Gus let her go.

"You're a good...guy...I mean...person. I...want to know...why. Was Grandpa Will a bad guy?" Gus started crying again.

She nodded. "Very bad."

"Why?"

"I don't know."

"Yes! You do. What...did he do? Why...did you murder him?" Gus never sounded so desperate. "Are you...a bad guy?"

What awful things filled his head? The thought that she could just up and kill her husband had worked him into a frenzy. What would Mo do? God, how Kate wished she were here. Everyone wants the truth until they know it.

Kate had gone as far as a mother could go to protect her daughter and wouldn't hesitate to do the same for Gus. She wanted him to think of her as good. Maybe it was the warmth of the campfire. Maybe the comfort of food in her belly. Probably the cough medicine sedated her better judgement. Likely, it was the lesson she'd learned years earlier that secrets never stay buried. What if Gus found out about his real father from someone else? He'd never forgive her.

"You know about sex and all that stuff, right?"

Gus rolled his eyes. "Yes...I do. Me...and Gloria... almost did it. Before...she dumped me."

"You know what incest is?" Kate blurted and immediately regretted it. Even from the grave, Will could fuck up her life.

Gus didn't look at her while he rolled his bottom lip over his top lip looking for the right answer. "Isn't it...when... like...a...ummm...brother and sister dog...have puppies together?" He looked at Kate, so innocent. Until now, the world's cruelty hadn't tainted him. That was all about to change, and Kate closed her eyes.

"Yes." She flopped backwards on the bedroll. A heaviness blanketed her. "And sometimes it happens with people. Sick people that don't understand it's not okay."

Gus didn't respond. He pulled the grate over the fire, then set a red coffee pot down on it. "I think...it's time for...cocoa."

Kate let the silence linger and hoped to hell this was the end of the rancid conversation.

"I'm confused," Gus admitted. "Maybe...I'm too... stupid...to understand."

Kate sat up. "No, Gus. I'm not explaining it very well because this is difficult for me and I don't like talking about what happened. But...you're right, you deserve the truth. And, I guess, it's best you hear it from me. So...I'm gonna tell you. But it's not nice. It's awful. You understand? It's going to hurt. Bad."

"I want...to know." Gus raised his voice and knelt next to Kate. His eyes pleading for the truth. "I can handle...it."

She couldn't look at him any longer and focused on the

tendrils of smoke escaping through the hole at the top of the teepee. "Will was my husband and your grandfather, and the reason I killed him was because he was also your father. He had sex with Em, so—I killed him. And I'd do it again if I had the chance." She waited before glancing at him for a reaction.

No discernible emotion showed on his face. He stood, brushed his knees off, then walked to the fire and stared into it. "My father...made a baby...with his own kid?" Gus crossed his arms. "And I am...that kid?"

"Yes." Kate watched Gus chew on the fact that he was a child of incest. "I am...like...the goofy barn kittens...that got born...because the mama cat...got bred...by her stupid father."

"What happened was bad. But that has nothing to do with you. You're living proof that something great can come from something awful. You're exactly like your mom." Kate stood and walked over. Put her hand on his shoulder. "Your mother was kind and caring and interesting, and smart— just like you, Gus. You make the world a better place, and I'm grateful to have you."

Gus buried his face in Kate's chest and cried. She held him tight, cradled and kissed his head and hoped she'd done the right thing.

"My father...was...a bad guy," he said between sobs.

"Yes."

Gus looked up. His red face wet with tears as he frowned and stepped away. "I'm glad...you killed him. Good guys...*should*...kill bad guys."

He filled a tin cup with hot water from the coffeepot and set it on a stump. From inside the cooler, he brought out a packet of cocoa powder. Without a word, he mixed up a cup of hot cocoa and offered it to Kate. Carefully, she took the steaming cup. "Thank you."

"Thank you...for telling...the truth."

"You know how much I love you?"

"A lot." It sounded more like a question than an answer.

"Bingo."

"I wish...all the...bad guys...would die."

"Me too, hon."

Gus sat on the edge of a stump as if he might need to bolt at any moment. He leaned toward the campfire and pulled off his hat. Ran his palm from the top of his head down over his forehead. He tossed two more logs onto the fire and huddled directly over it. Orange and black shadows danced on his face. He seemed to have the weight of the world on his shoulders as Kate sipped hot cocoa and resisted the urge to sleep. Walter snored.

"Wonder how long it'll take them to get here?" Kate asked

Gus went to his backpack and dug out his Magic 8 Ball. He put the ball next to his mouth, whispered something, shook it, and stopped. With the ball cradled in both hands, he watched and waited.

"Without a doubt," Gus said, taking a moment before shaking the ball again.

"Are you sure?" He righted the ball. His eyes and mouth opened wide as he read the magical answer. "Definitely." Gus nodded his head and sighed. "Okay. I will...do it."

"What are you doing?" Kate asked and slurped.

"I'm gonna...go...watch for them." Gus shoved his glasses and backpack on and went outside.

Kate set the cup on the ground. Stretched her arms as the muscles in her aching back pulled. Walter rolled over. She yawned, laid back on the bedroll, and snuggled in next to Walter. The powerful scent of pine oozed from his ear. Telling Gus the truth might have been the right thing to do, she told herself, but it weighed heavily on her heart. The last thing she wanted to do was stomp on his innocence. The world would beat that out of him soon enough. Something pulled at her. Sucking her down like an invisible force through the bedroll and into the earth. She curled into the fetal position and closed her eyes for a moment.

Chapter Nine

A spectacular harvest moon climbed above Devil's Nose but it didn't impress Gus one bit. For over two weeks, he'd studied the moon's phases and had been looking forward to seeing the magnificent orange moon at its fullest. But now, after all the truth, it seemed nothing much mattered. More nights than not, Gus stared into space, thinking about how the moon pulled not only at the ocean, but also at the rock under his boots. Earth's surface worked like the tides, just not as obvious. Sometimes at night, he'd leave his teepee, crawl into his hammock, and watch without blinking until the shadowy face of the moon became familiar. The moon was underrated and unappreciated. Gus worried about what would happen to life on Earth since learning that the moon had been drifting away like everyone he'd ever loved.

The truth brought back that familiar, terrible, wicked feeling. Like he wanted to punch someone. He made a fist and imagined punching Gloria's ugly boyfriend, Homer, right in the face. Gloria would be mad if he hurt Homer.

His heart banged harder and harder in his chest until something strangled him and he couldn't breathe.

He ran to a sapling spruce and squeezed his fist around the tiny tender needles, milking the little limb. Rubbing the greens together in his hands, he covered his nose with his palms and inhaled the smell of Christmas. Christmas always made him happy. Not this time. This time, even the smell of Christmas couldn't fix the hurt.

At the creek, Gus knelt, staring into the black water. He took a deep breath, then sunk his head underwater to drown the panic. Underwater, the cold shocked his system into survival mode as he counted to ten in his head, just like Miss Mo had taught him, but he could not drown out all the bad things in his life. The badness grew like an abscess. Painful and infected.

When he came up for air, the abscess broke and Gus knew he was unfixable this time. He'd felt the crack just before the thing inside him burst. Probably his heart. The pain was worse than when you get your fingers caught in the car door. This pain lasted longer and could not be soothed with ice or ibuprofen or even a popsicle. He needed Gloria. She could soothe his hurt.

"Gloria," Gus whispered. "Gloria." She'd busted his heart into a bunch of jagged pieces that stabbed him every time he thought of her with Homer. All because she'd gotten a job at the Dollar General in West Point and said she liked her new boss, Homer. At first, Gus was glad to hear it, because Gloria hated everyone. Getting along with people was one thing that Gloria was terrible at. Breaking up was the other. She'd sent Gus a text message that read: *Homer is my boyfriend now not you. Don't call or text me no more!*

Gus obeyed. He cried and cried until his mom called and scheduled an appointment with Maureen Yamaguchi.

82

It took about ten sessions with Miss Mo before Gus could eat or sleep or go into the Dollar General. It thrilled Gus when Gloria and her stupid fat Homer quit the Dollar General and began growing weed for a guy named Red. Now, at least he could go in and buy hot dogs, Fritos, Cheez Whiz, and his favorite gummy worms whenever he wanted without having to look at Homer. Homer had to be the dumbest name Gus had ever heard of. What kind of mother or father would name a kid Homer?

This time the pain and bad stuff made Gus mad. This time he didn't want to die. He had to live, and stood. Stepped away from the creek, and realized he had a goal. A purpose to live. Angry fists punched the air. First, he had to save Miss Mo. Second, he'd kill every bad guy like his stupid biological father. The Magic 8 Ball said he should do it. The ball had never been wrong. Plus, if he didn't do it, who the heck would?

Someone had to be brave enough to make the world a better place. Grammy Kate was brave. But she was sick and too tired to do much more tonight. It was up to him. The memory hit with a vengeance and would not let up. "I won't…blow it…this time." He hoped he wouldn't run and hide like he had the last time he'd had the chance to be a brave hero.

The day after someone shot his pet buffalo, Gus fell apart. He had to see Gloria, but she was at her boss Dustin's. The house sat at the end of a long dirt road—mostly uphill. Too many trees made it feel dark and creepy and cold. Gus zipped up his puffy coat as high as it would go. The ragged house was faded like the yellowed Polaroids that his mom kept in a shoebox. Three rusted cars and dogs on chains cluttered the yard. All the dogs got mad when Gus walked up. A silver pit bull with blue eyes growled from under the steps, and the whole porch shook when he jerked against his chain. Gloria and her friend Nicole sat on a torn couch on Dustin's porch, trimming weed into a plastic bowl, and Gloria jumped up and threw a shovel at the barking dog. That shut him up. Gus stepped onto the porch and kissed Gloria on the cheek. Nicole made gagging sounds, got up, and sat on the steps to trim more buds.

"You're supposed to ask permission before you touch someone! That includes kissing," Gloria had said with her angry bird face.

"Can I have a kiss, please?" Gus leaned closer to her face and used his irresistible smile to persuade her. She let him kiss her twice on the cheek and once on the lips. Gus felt better. "I have to…go to…the bathroom." Gus opened the screen door.

"Dustin don't like anyone in the house. Go find a tree," Nicole said.

Gus jumped off the porch, and the dogs barked. They were mad because they had a terrible life and Gus wished he could unleash them. Let them run through the forest—happy and free. Junk cars stunk like burned popcorn as he passed. It took a while to find a safe place to pee out of sight. Gus's pee steamed and so did his breath while he whistled "Jingle Bells."

A girl screamed as Gus zipped up. He ran back toward the house, where three guys with big guns ran up the porch.

"Calaveras Sheriff's Department! Hands up!" someone yelled over the barking dogs. Gus turned and ran away because guns scared him back then. Spiderwebs stuck to his face, and he could not breathe. It felt like spiders were crawling all over his head, and he swatted and slapped them. A hefty branch ripped a hole in the front of his new puffy coat. Feathers shot out and scattered like a flock of spooked geese. He squeezed his eyes closed for a long, long time and wanted to scream because he was a total chicken. There had to be a way to be brave and save Gloria.

In the house, Gloria, Nicole, and Dustin were lined up on their stomachs on the living room floor when Gus walked in, their hands pinned behind their backs with plastic zip ties. Black storage boxes stacked behind them— almost to the ceiling. The place smelled like skunks lived there instead of people. Three white guys with haircuts you get in the army looked at him.

"What the hell?" The oldest guy turned around fast and aimed a big gun at Gus. His shriveled face turned as red as his hair. It was funny, but Gus did not laugh. "Where did you come from?" Red asked, looking like he wanted to kill someone. Gus got scared and nervous and sick all at the same time, and sat down in a lawn chair. "You best not move," Red said.

"Please do not arrest Gloria." Gus stood up. "She is innocent."

"No one here is innocent, including you." Red smiled, but he wasn't happy. He shoved Gus down into the lawn chair. "Shut the fuck up."

Nicole wheezed and coughed, but the guy standing over her did not care; he took her cellphone out of her back pocket. Something about the way his legs bowed reminded Gus of a bull rider when he stepped over Nicole to Gloria. He frisked her too, but all he found was a pack of gummy bears in her sweatshirt. His Wranglers were too tight, and he could barely fit the pack in his back pocket. Police would not take your gummy bears. His cowboy boots were ripped along the sides, and when he straddled Dustin, one hole opened up like a big mouth. "No wallet— no firearm," he said, and held Dustin's cellphone overhead like a trophy. "Weed ain't worth dyin' for, is it, Dustin?" Red asked.

"No, sir. Take it all." Dustin sounded terrified.

Red slammed his gun into Dustin's back. "Need the cash too, bud."

"What cash?" Dustin was on the verge of tears.

Red hit him again, but this time, he also kicked him. Gus wished he and Gloria were at her trailer eating her gummy bears and kissing.

"Okay!" Dustin screamed. "In the dog food bag next to the fridge!"

"I wanna see your badge!" Gloria rolled onto her back, but everyone ignored her. "None a you gots badges! You ain't *even* cops!" Gloria was smart, and that was why Gus loved her.

A guy with big muscles and big pimples came from the back of the house with a bunch of guns. "Look what I found." He had four big guns in his arms like a load of firewood and took them outside.

"Good work, Sarge," Red said. He told the Bullrider to "dump the dog food next to the fridge—see if you find a prize."

The sack of dog food sounded like a load of gravel being dumped. Dustin said a very, very bad word. He said lots of bad words and banged his head on the floor until Bullrider came in carrying a SpongeBob lunch box. When he opened it, he found money instead of lunch. A lot of money.

Sarge opened the screen door and poked his head in. "I'll load the weed and we be gone."

Red took the lunch box, and Gloria kicked him where the sun does not shine. "My cousins are gonna kill you buttholes." Only Gloria did not say *butt*.

Red yelped like a pup when you pick it up by the neck. The lunch box hit the floor when he grabbed his nuts. Sarge ran to Gloria, and she screamed when he snatched her hair. It hurt Gus's ears and he screamed. When she kicked the plastic table full of dirty dishes over, they seemed to crash in on Gus's head.

Gloria flopped around like a fish out of water and got away from Sarge. She was strong, another reason Gus loved her, but when Sarge stomped on her stomach, she did not fight anymore. He dragged her by her feet into the hall, and Gus had to do something fast.

Anger made Gus brave. He stood up, and without thinking it through, grabbed the lunch box and ran out the door. Dogs barked and rattled their chains as soon as Gus leaped off the porch. He slid past the crazy silver dog and made it under the stairs. The slide was perfect! Better than all the ones Coach Bryan made him do during baseball practice last spring.

"That fat little fucker is fast." It sounded like the Bull-rider was on the porch.

"He has a disorder or something," said Red. "Chill, I'll find him."

Under the house, the air tasted like wet dirt. Gus was suffocating. On the brink of death, he wriggled deeper and deeper, like a trout when they leave your hand and disappear into the darkness. His heart pounded, and he squeezed the handle on the lunch box. Time got all messed up, and he did not know if he'd been in the narrow crawl space for five minutes or five hours until sunlight coming through the slats at the back of the house stopped him. Sweat slithered down his face, but he shivered.

Stealing the money would not save Gloria. Another stupid move. Gus never knew that he'd made a bad decision until long after he'd made it. His heart shook when Red's work boots appeared and he said, "August, come out please."

"Sorry, Red." Gus said it over and over as he crawled out from under the house. The dogs barked so loudly he did not know if Red could hear him. "I am sorry!" He stood and offered Red his best irresistible smile and handed over the lunch box. With his enormous hand, Red grabbed Gus's puffy coat and dang near yanked him off his feet. Feathers flew from the hole, and Gus wanted to scream. He would never be brave. Never be the hero. And worst of all, never save Gloria. "I'm… sorry…Red." Gus looked down at the red clay and dried dog turds. "I got scared…and confused. I had to…to save…Gloria." He knew he'd never live down the painful truth.

Thinking back, his failure to be brave was probably why Gloria dumped him. Armed with the brutal truth might help him be brave. It wasn't the truth he'd wanted or could have ever imagined, but Grammy Kate gave it to him and he had to handle it. No better ways to deal with the pain and anger than the thought of killing bad guys, and eating Fritos.

The half-full bag of Fritos inside the ice chest tasted delicious. Gus ate to power up and remembered the quote his mom had embroidered on lace and framed for him. It hung next to the mirror above the dresser in Gus's bedroom before the bank made them move. *Know thyself and you need not fear 100 battles.* Mom had paraphrased the quote when she gave Gus *The Art of War.* The book had left a lasting impression. Especially the chapter about knowing your enemy.

Gus watched Benny nibble at the ground in case he'd missed something. *Know thy enemy*—it was as important as knowing thyself. Gus knew his enemy very well. He tipped the Frito bag over his open mouth—shaking greasy remnants onto his tongue.

He stomped back inside the teepee. Grammy Kate slept on her side next to Walter. Gus pulled a wool blanket from behind his bedroll and covered them.

Quietly, he worked the walkie talkie into his backpack and slipped it on. After taking time to dry his hair by the fire and feeding himself two more hot dogs, Gus picked up a piece of broken charcoal from his drawing collection piled alongside the firepit. With it, he left Grammy Kate a message next to the door flap, strapped on his headlamp, and left to prove he could be brave.

PART II
Chapter Ten

I drifted in and out of a dark, howling rainstorm that clawed and whipped at me with tentacles. Dread paralyzing my urge to run. Pelting rain so angry and loud it hurt my head as I floated somewhere between conscious and not. My eyelids stuck, locked down tight as clamshells. An extraordinarily vivid and lengthy hypnopompic hallucination fled as I floundered and swayed to wake, to see. Pain stabbed like a spear shot down through the apex of my skull.

Smoke and something akin to burning flesh festered and nauseated me. About to erupt, I tried to open my eyes. One lid cracked, but saw only darkness. The other eye refused to budge. Something was stuck over my eyes and pulling my bangs. I squinted and tried to bring my arms to my face, but they too were stuck. My heart thrashed and throbbed as panic set in. In spite of my best effort, I could not free my arms from behind me. Wet saturated my eyes and face. Rain. No. More likely tears. I recognized the taste of salt.

Clotted blood slithered down the back of my throat. I couldn't open my mouth. Something kept my lips from moving.

My nose itched and I wiggled it up and down, then side to side. The tug of whatever blindfolded me loosened its grip. I scrunched my eyes tight and worked my cheeks up as if I were a happy, smiling fool. The stickiness weakened its grip. With my cheek against my shoulder, I rubbed over and over until the tape peeled away from one eye.

A forest closed in—smothering me. Sitting on the ground, I was dry. There was no rain, only confusion. Wind —terribly loud and cold—filled with smoke. A campfire. Flames too far away to warm me.

The sound I mistook for rain came from a man in filthy jeans two sizes too big for him. A mouth-breather who stood nearby stirring something in a pan. It sizzled. A propane stove sat on a table created from a long flat rock. Two cedar stumps on either end served as sturdy legs.

Treetops shuddered and fired pine needles down like slow bullets. I shivered without feeling cold—sitting on bare ground with my legs outstretched. No shoes, only socks. Why? Where were my shoes? I couldn't feel my feet or my legs. Everything except my aching head was numb. Where were my things? My backpack? My phone? I looked at my pants pocket where my phone should be. Gone.

All of a sudden I knew I would die. I'd been doing my utmost to live my best life and will have failed spectacularly. Would death be easier to accept if I'd left a positive impact on the world? Would my life or my death matter had I made a difference? I wanted a second chance more than my next breath.

The man turned. Looked at me with surprise. "Uh-oh." His expression hid under a bushy black beard. "You see me." He shook his head, shrugged, and stepped away from the stove. A carcass of some sort hung from a branch behind the stove. Big. Blood red. Sinew. Fibrous muscle along bone. It appeared to be a leg. At the bottom swung a hoof.

The man stood in front of me. He'd replaced his camo ballcap with my San Francisco Giants hat. He knelt— offering a folded tortilla with scorched muscle and fat inside. A thick gold crucifix hung from around his neck as he peeled the tape from my lips.

"No screaming," he said.

"Owww," I mumbled.

"Hungry?" He held the steaming food to my mouth. "Is good." He took a bite, possibly to prove he wasn't trying to poison me. When he returned it to my lips, I turned away and gagged. Producing nothing but tears. Where was I? Who was this man and why feed me? The lack of compre-hension fed on itself as my confusion grew along with the shooting pain in my head and face.

The man nodded and peeled away the dangling tape now only clinging to my temple. "You have a bad gash." He tilted my head with his grubby hand and inspected me. "Is not bleeding no more." He stood and walked away as I attempted to open my freed eye. It wouldn't budge.

Memory always has its way and mine was fickle as it returned in increments. Fragments of fishing. Running. Fleeing something. Someone. Someone chasing me. I was scared. Terrified really. Walter. My heart sank. Poor sweet Walter. The man's face, his black beard before everything went blank.

The man with the black beard was a voracious eater. Sick and weak, I tried to stand, but my arms were bound around the tree behind me. I tugged, pulled hard, struggling with all of my might to free myself as the man watched and ate.

A scream emerged and almost erupted before I forced it down. Screaming in fear is nothing more than noise. It serves the purpose of sharpening focus in the face of a threat as well as a warning to others but was completely useless in my current situation. A scream goes straight from the ear to the amygdala, the part of the brain that processes fear and kickstarts the body's fight-or-flight response. Both futile at this point. Fear would only hinder the possibility of an idea and irritate my captor.

I had to keep my wits about me and use the skills I'd acquired over my years in practice. Coming to terms with the fact that I was being held hostage would theoretically advance my survival. Good. Presumably, if he wanted to kill me, I'd already be dead. Early in my career I'd assisted the San Francisco Police Department in several successful hostage negotiations. First, I knew to slow my mind and my racing heart. I sucked in a deep, calming breath and exhaled. Took in my surroundings and more calming breaths one after another.

Two camo-colored tarps hung tight but flapped between a half-dozen conifers—roofing the camp. A green tent trembled in the wind ten feet from a smoldering campfire. Burlap bundles, each about the size of a throw pillow, were secured in duct tape and stacked at least five feet high and twelve-feet long. The entire thing resembled a sandbag wall reminiscent of a World War II film. The wall stood under protective brown tarps.

Marijuana. It had to be. Growing weed in a National Forest is a federal offense. All this because Walter and I were in the wrong place at the wrong time. Sorrow at my predicament and losing Walter sidetracked me for a long, sickening moment. Recalling the next step in hostage nego-tiations was impossible as I leaned back against the bark, tilted my head up, and without overthinking, spoke.

"My name is Maureen Yamaguchi. My friends call me Mo." I said it as if I truly had friends.

The man disconnected a small propane canister from the two-burner camp stove.

"I'm very sorry my dog, Walter, scared you."

The man threw the old green canister underhand. It disappeared somewhere in the darkness. He glared at me.

"Walter had a difficult life before I adopted him, and sometimes it shows. I know you didn't want to shoot him," I said, wishing I could move my body to elaborate. Only seven percent of communication is verbal. The fastest way to build rapport is through body language, something I'd practiced with every patient. I tucked my chin to my chest and shook my head.

The man retrieved a fresh propane canister from a card-board box on the ground.

"I suspect you've had a difficult life as well." I smiled as he spun the canister into place on the stove. The propane hissed and he burped. "It must be terrible living out here all summer. The mosquitos alone would send me running home. Where's home for you?"

He looked at me, scratched his bearded jaw, and crossed his arms. "Home—" he said.

A woman approached from the tent. My first inclination was to connect with her. "Hello? I'm Maureen. Mo."

She appeared to be in her twenties and stout. She came toward me in a hurry, with a roll of duct tape in her hand. Long black hair like a veil hung well past her shoulders. Her beefy face poked with scabs and what appeared to be bug bites among a crop of red pimples. When she knelt in front of me and shoved her face into mine, her big brown eyes popped as she screamed. "Idiot! Why is her eyes uncovered?" She shot the man a disgusted look then glared back at me. I could smell the booze through her peppermint gum. She tore a strip of duct tape with her fangs.

"I understand you're angry. You have every right—"

She slapped the strip of tape over my mouth. "That'll shut you up a while!" She looked at me and ripped another section of tape and doubled it over my mouth. "You really fucked up, didn't you?" She crossed her arms as if waiting for a response.

"Hear me?" she asked, and I nodded. The man shook his head and ate from the pan on the stove.

"Should have let you die," she growled at me through a clenched jaw.

The man clicked his tongue and wagged his finger—no. "More trouble for you." As if he were the authority.

The woman eyed me. If it were up to her, I'd be dead. Suddenly, she seemed to soften. A smiled cracked her face and for a split second I felt a connection before her hiking boot slammed full-force into my abdomen. She strolled away as if kicking someone in the stomach was no big deal. I fought for breath. A fish on the shore, gulping for tiny bits of precious air.

I'd had the wind knocked out of me before. Once, in the seventh grade. Rosemary Rivera wanted to beat my ass after school. Rather than fight her—I ran. Ran for my life, pushing past crowds of classmates the minute the bell rang. My feet slapped and echoed down the long hallway. I'd made it two blocks before Rosemary and her gang caught me. Without explanation, Rosemary chose me to brutalize that day and slammed her fist so deep into my stomach it seemed it went straight through me and out the other side. I fell to my knees and curled into a fetal position. Everyone laughed until my pathetic sobbing no longer entertained them. They left me curled on the park path crying. I'd always wished that at the very least I'd attempted to fight back.

Perhaps the full moon had created the threat of impending doom, but I decided right then and there that this time I would fight back. Being a cooperative victim had haunted me for far too long. For months, I suffered through irrational and intense fear. Rosemary made sleeping impossible and I studied her like I'd studied math and English, yet failed to comprehend how the girl had obtained her power. How had she become the leader of the pack? She wasn't smart or pretty or rich. She had no special talents other than her ability to apply thick black eyeliner with precision, and a propensity for violence.

A brief study on bullies helped me understand that Rosemary's behavior was the only way she could establish social dominance. It was all the girl had—perhaps all she wanted out of life. My fear of Rosemary soon turned to empathy, and then an obsession that eventually included thick eyeliner. My mother found it hilarious—said that Japanese eyes were not suitable for makeup. I laughed it off and wore the liner for one week until the day I found the nerve to follow Rosemary home from school.

When she entered the Second Chance Homeless Shelter, I waited and watched from across the street. Twenty minutes later Rosemary emerged and crossed the street. I smiled as she approached. "Hi, Rosemary. What a pleasant coincidence running into you here."

Rosemary shoved me—hard. "Quit following me you fucking lezbo!" She grabbed my hair with both hands and threw me down. The first punch to the face stung my nose.

The second hurt but numbed my face enough that I hardly felt the third. When the urge to fight back finally came, Rosemary was gone and I was bleeding.

It was practically impossible to read, let alone wear eyeliner, with two swollen and blackened eyes. I refused to go to school—for equal parts fear and embarrassment. During the day, the city library was the perfect place to hide and dissect myself. Was I attracted to Rosemary? Could I possibly be gay? I'd never had a boyfriend and was already in the seventh grade. Most girls had French-kissed a boy and some went all the way, or at least that was the rumor. I'd never even held hands with a boy.

I studied stacks of psychology books and discovered why I was targeted. It all came down to my lack of aggression and how I became visibly upset when persecuted. I had no friends to intervene and I assumed a high level of fear when threatened. The perfect victim. My attraction to Rosemary had not been sexual—only an irrational and misplaced subconscious desire to be like her. Strong and admired.

Bound and muted under the cedar with no way to utilize my abilities, I hoped that somewhere out there my only friend Kate would use hers. Deep in the forest I made a conscious decision and refused to accept the role or fate of the victim. I studied my surroundings down to the most minute detail. The large bone handle knife that hung in a leather sheath from the man's belt. Tarps. Tent. A makeshift bed below a tarp covered in boughs. The camp kitchen and trash piled just beyond. The distinct scent of skunk that must be ripe cannabis buds. Prayer candle burning on a single stump like a shrine, the glowing saint painted on the glass resembling an amalgamation of the Virgin Mary and the Grim Reaper.

The man gathered whatever was in the skillet with a

tortilla and rolled it. He pinched it between his thumb and forefinger as he came toward me. This time when he offered food I nodded. Slowly, he scratched at the corner of the duct tape and peeled it back. As the food neared, I reached out for it like a baby bird and bit. It was hot and good—and I wondered why they hadn't killed me as I chewed. Why bother feeding me? They were growers, not killers. Summer was over and the weather had changed which meant growing had probably concluded. They just needed to transport their crop. Perhaps my captors and myself harbored the same hopes and fears. Stay put, stay quiet, until we're done and we can all go on our merry ways. Wait it out restrained to the tree.

I hadn't noticed my hunger until the second bite and hardly chewed before swallowing the meat. Being a vegetarian for the past thirty years, I wondered how my body would react to consuming meat again. The last bite went down fast and I considered asking for more, but thought better of it. The man patted me on the head like an obedient dog before retrieving a bottle of water from the makeshift granite table. He unscrewed the cap and offered it. I nodded and he held the bottle against my lips. Greedily, I sucked and gulped until the entire thing was empty.

"Ibuprofen?" I asked in the sweetest voice possible.

The man twisted, then squished the plastic bottle in his hands and cast it off in the general direction of the trash pile. He reached down to replace the tape.

"Please. No. I can't breathe. My nose is swollen. Please. I'll be quiet. I promise. Please." I spoke just above a whisper. "It's so difficult to breathe."

The man walked away, leaving the tape dangling from my right cheek. He sat near the fire and watched me.

I closed my eyes. How had I ended up in this nightmare? I should have stayed in San Francisco where one expected an attack. At least you're on your toes when aware of the criminal activity in the city. Moving to Calaveras County, I'd let my guard down and might pay the ultimate price. Adapting to rural life had been fairly easy until now. I loved the fact I could leave home and be alone on walks or a bike ride—a perk that wasn't possible in the city.

Life in the country lacked sidewalks, street lights, traffic, Uber, buses, trains and most of the time, electricity and cell service. There were no places to shop, eat, have my hair or nails done—forget having a massage—and worst of all, no one to deliver my gluten-free vegetarian pizza. In spite of the lack of conveniences, and the need for four-wheel drive, I loved it. Loved the deer that roamed, the ravens that barked, and the bears that left fat prints in the snow. Most of all, I loved feeling that I'd brought help to a community desperate for it. Folks who'd never had the opportunity for behavioral health services. I loved believing I'd made a difference in someone's life. But somehow doubt had always crept in.

"I have to pee," I said.

The man stood, lifted his brow and palms, then shrugged before returning to the cooking area.

"Please. Por favor. Banos." I pleaded.

"Um—Lupeee," the man yelled as he sealed the package of tortillas and placed them into a plastic ice chest. He marched to the tent. "Hey!"

Lupe sprang from the nylon flap and the man recoiled. She caught him with a fisted slap, knocking my ballcap off his head. He held his cheek and cowered as she cursed him in a groggy voice and fiery gestures. I assumed she was angry because the man had used her name. Lupe. He looked like a pudgy child being reprimanded by his evil stepmother. Lupe was indeed the jefe here and continued cursing him about the lady tied to the tree. I pieced the words together and could comprehend the gist of it.

"No." She raised her index finger. "Better being late on delivery than this, no?"

"Red can take her. Is his problem."

Lupe laughed. "You're the problem. When he sees you brought her here." Lupe crossed her arms and shook her head. "The bitch can ID us now. People will be looking for her. They'll come here! I'm *not* going back to jail." She ducked into her tent while the man picked my cap up off the ground. Before dusting it off, he stared at it a long while, then slowly put it on his head. He pulled the brim down hard and approached.

His dark eyes locked on me as he stood, legs spread, scratching at the scruffy growth on his face. His cheek still burned red where she'd hit him. I thought about apologizing, then thought better of it. Apologizing would only put me at a disadvantage. By accepting responsibility for Lupe's wrath, the man could transfer blame to me. He was embarrassed about being belittled even if only in front of a captive audience. I refused to look away and held his gaze straight-faced until he disappeared behind my cedar.

His footsteps faded, but no matter which way I turned my aching head, or moved my throbbing eye, I could not see him. My brain was a pulsating mass ready to explode. Probably a concussion, but not life-threatening if I could only stay awake. My ribs ripped at my nerve endings and I hoped they were only bruised and not broken. Worst of all was the biting cold and the excruciating urge to pee. I could piss my pants, but that would cause me to be even colder. I closed my eyes and forced a grin. Living in denial had always been my best defense.

It wasn't easy—overriding the current nightmare that I prayed was merely an extended hypnopompic hallucination, with imagery of a happy place. Floating on my back in the warm Pacific Ocean. The gentle current rocking me like a precious child. Not a cloud in the sky. Only the comfort of blue sunshine and the satisfaction of having learned to swim. I drifted. A deep sense of rebirth washed over me. Then breath—breathing suddenly felt luxurious—louder. Breathing harder and harder until something yanked me back. I sank fast.

Chapter Eleven

Ripped from the tranquility I'd created and back to the cold dark night. The man's breathing became alarmingly loud and carried traces of cigarette smoke. Behind the tree he pulled my arms, then my wrists. His fingers touched mine and after a few brief tugs my arms fell. He stepped out from behind the tree with a skinning knife in his hand.

My numb arms quivered forward like broken wings and I rubbed my wrists, duct tape still attached to my left. The man reached down, grabbed my hand, and pulled me to my feet—smiling, as if we were in on the same joke.

"Go." He tossed his chin up. Did this mean go, you're free? Get out of here? I wondered until he said, "No running," and held the knife up to confirm the warning, then pointed it at the dark woods, as if to say, After you ma'am. Perhaps he'd gotten into a situation with the cartel that he could not get out of. Odds were, he was a low-level hardworking farmer who'd worked all summer to make someone else rich. He'd made a terrible mistake by attempting to either pilfer a bit for himself or deliver during the day—according to Lupe. Walter and I had simply been in the wrong place at the wrong time.

Sticks, pine needles, jagged rocks, and sharp little pinecones stabbed at the soles of my feet through my socks. The man's dirty fingers gripped my bicep as we hiked upwards, too far for a simple bathroom break. I buried the fear swelling in my mind and considered running. Or throwing myself off the first ledge I found. A massive slab of granite protruded like a giant puzzle piece atop the treed hillside. Perfectly sized and placed for landing a Search and Rescue helicopter, I thought.

The man escorted me up a sloped section of the rock and stopped. From his back pocket he produced a long piece of cheap yellow rope. He clenched my wrist as he wrapped one end of the rope around it, then secured it with a clove hitch.

"Pee." He released my wrist, but held to the opposite end of the rope like a leash.

"Here?" My high tone failed to conceal my fear.

The man moved behind me and brought both arms behind my back. A tar-like body odor slithered up my swollen nose. I held my breath as he tethered my wrists together painfully tight.

"Please," I said softly. "I just want to relieve myself. I won't attempt to escape. I swear. You can trust me." I assured him with images of us returning to camp, sitting around the fire, and eventually sharing secrets like old friends.

He stepped in front of me. His crucifix shone in the moonlight as he snatched up the waistband of my pants and unbuttoned them.

"God's watching you." My mind and heart raced.

He didn't answer. Didn't look at me. A grin cracked his hairy face as he slid my zipper down.

"I can't..." I tore away from him and bolted over the flat rock. Running as if my life depended on it. My pants fell to my ankles, shackling me as I headed for the cover of darkness and thick forest downhill. Pants strangling my stride and hands bound behind my back, made outrunning the man impossible. He'd soon catch me, so I dropped to a prone position behind a downed and dead cedar. Alongside the rotting log, I burrowed in with all my might, trying to disappear into the damp earth.

Buried in sticky mountain misery, a branch jabbed through my underwear and prodded my inner thigh. Fear and adrenaline cremated the cold while my heart punched my torso. With the tang of the mountain misery on my tongue, I breathed through my mouth and sank my face deep into the undergrowth, rubbing and working the duct tape off my cheek. Slow down. Quiet, I told myself. It's safe here. My thrumming heartbeat made listening for his approach impossible. Time slowed. Silence took over and rang in my ears. I shook uncontrollably—my body's reaction to the rush of adrenaline.

Working my pants off with my feet in case I had to run was an option, but a risk I couldn't take. Any movement could sacrifice my cover. Just be still. Not daring to breathe, I pictured a quail as bird dogs approached. Don't fly. Don't fly. My head spun and vertigo forced me onto my side. Slowly, I wiggled my back and butt against the downed log. Spooning with nature might have been insightful had it been a conscious decision in a peaceful situation. At the most inopportune time, I thought of Kate. If she could see me now. I wished I'd told her the truth. Anger scrubbed regret from my mind.

Heat, then sweat, burned like fire from the inside out. I tried hard to swallow the nausea, but my mouth was too dry. My tongue became mummified and motionless as I heaved up every bit of meat and tortilla. The grunts and retching would surely announce my whereabouts. I turned over, struggling against my pant shackles and shoved my mouth as deep into the brushy mountain misery as possible. Vomit warmed my cheeks. A whiff of my own putrid stench blurred my eyes. I lifted my head.

Had he heard me? I blinked away tears. My heart did that familiar flip before I understood why. Volatile molecules had met with receptors in my nose. One synapse signaled my amygdala, the hippocampus, and triggered fight or flight. Tar. The smell sharp as a razor made my skin crawl. I'd smelled him before his black hiking boots stepped into focus.

He towered above me, smiling down like he'd won. Like it was all a sick game of hide and seek. He spun my Giants cap around backwards on his head. Powered by rage, I rolled onto my back, reared, and drove both feet at him. I aimed for his scrotum, but his paunch took the hit. The man gasped as he bent and grabbed his stomach.

"I'll kill you!" I'd never spoken those words—never wanted or needed to. Anger suspended my pain. How could this be happening, I wondered. It seemed so unreal. In my fifties, flat-chested, and beginning to resemble my grandfather, most men did not find me attractive. But I knew better. I'd treated enough rape victims and dealt with two rapists. I knew the act had nothing whatsoever to do with sex. For this man, it was about control and the power he needed to regain after Lupe had ridiculed him. Once again, I was merely a convenient opportunity.

I attempted to roll away, but the beast stomped the air

out of my back, then wedged some sort of material in my mouth. With my tongue, I tried and tried to force it out because breathing through my swollen nose was nearly impossible. I was suffocating and desperate for air. Nothing else mattered. Only my next breath. Breathe.

Slowly oxygen hissed up one nostril and offered life as the man latched onto my ankles, then my pants. Before I could stop him, he'd yanked them away. I rolled from my side onto my back in time to see him drop my pants and unzip his. I scooched backwards as he rubbed his growing erection and seemed to struggle for an approach. Surrounded by tall trees—an audience of perverted voyeurs. The moment he bent, I fired both feet, but failed to connect.

The man's eyes narrowed and in less than a heartbeat he flipped me onto my stomach. His weight landed on me like being hit, then pinned under a car.

I couldn't move. Couldn't breathe anything other than the pungent stench of hot tar that clung to him.

Terror prevented my devising an escape. His nails scratched my hips as he ripped my underwear down. My arms would surely dislocate from my shoulders at any moment. All I could do was wiggle. I thought I heard him spit. This is going to happen if you don't do something, the voice in my head screamed.

He stroked and pushed, trying to force himself inside without benefit of an erection. His hand guiding as he went. Hot tobacco-laced breath upon my neck.

I dropped my head. His head and torso came down, closing in on me with each stroke as he neared penetration. An animalistic anger emerged in me.

As the man thrust again, I shook and released my inner demons. Energized by an unfamiliar power, I used my head

—threw it backwards with all my might. Full force—the back of my skull slamming into his. The crack was like nothing I'd ever heard. Breaking of bone and brittle freedom so loud I felt it in my soul.

Gasping and gagging, my heavy breathing became growls as I writhed and slithered and floundered out from under the limp man. I knelt next to his plump buttock. His penis planted in the dirt. I wasted no time backing my bound hands against the knife sheath at his hip. Fingering the knife from the sheath was awkward. It took what seemed like forever to unstrap, but what else could I do? I fumbled to position the knife once I had it in my hands. The thing was razor-sharp. Grasping the handle with both hands, I stood and backed up until I felt the log at the back of my thighs. Using my weight to push the tip of the blade deep into the rotting wood, it sank with little effort. I sawed at the rope around my wrists.

The beast inside the man snorted while I worked to free myself. Pushing and pulling the ties against the blade. Suddenly free, I ripped the knife away without taking my eyes off the man. Yanked the wadded material from my mouth and filled my lungs with wonderful breaths—one after another. With the weapon in my hand, I stood above him.

How would it feel to bury the knife in his back, or better yet simply run the razor-sharp blade along his jugular? He moved his arms and turned his head. That's when I grabbed the tree limb that had been tormenting me while I hid. He rolled over and I gripped the limb in my dominant right hand.

Small holes opened up in my memory, then slammed shut. It wouldn't be the first time I'd killed someone. But this time it would be intentional. This time I was sober and not behind the wheel. This time my victim wasn't innocent.

Way past the middle of nowhere, half-naked in the dark forest, my savage beast stirred. I swung the limb like an ax and chopped twice at the man's head. My ballcap bounced, but stayed put on his head. He didn't move. I waited until he grunted like the pig he was and I bashed him again. Then twice more because I'd become the savage beast. Growling with each blow.

When the limb broke, I dropped it.

"Fuck you—you fuck!" It was the first time I'd used such foul language. If a woman screams in the forest and there is no one there to hear it, does she make a sound? "Fuck you!" I took back my hat, but my wounded head hurt too much to put it on.

My underwear clung to the man's filthy fingers. I lifted the pudgy hand and it was as if a massive weight had been lifted. I could breathe, but not quiet the irresistible impulse, and held the hand higher. Dirt ringed the wrinkles on his wrist as I moved the tip of the blade against the vein. Considered pressing harder until I'd slit the radial artery length wise, and then I'd sever it crossways before the heavy bleeding began. A perfect crucifix—the same cut two of my patients had used.

"Homie." It was Lupe's voice. Fear tempered, then replaced my rage. I dropped the hand and my hat, snatched up my underwear, and stepped into them as fast as humanly possible, as vengeance shifted to survival. My pants were at the base of a sapling.

"Aye Homie!"

I ran to my pants and had them in my hand when a beam of light stabbed the dark like swords swiping at me. A shot rang out—simultaneously a flash came from the flat rock. Bits of log splintered and slapped my bare legs. By the time it registered that I was being shot at, a second flash came. The round so close that I heard and felt the buzz of a bullet whizz past my ear. *Runnn*, it seemed to say.

Another shot pierced the night as I ran. Adrenaline masked the pain in my feet as I escaped, snaking my way through a stand of cedars scattered in shadows and moonlight. Refusing to slow down, I hurried through the forest until it ended abruptly and the ground disappeared. The lack of evergreens exposed a full moon and the severe drop below.

Chapter Twelve

Yellow moonglow lit the way as Gus rode Benny bareback. His legs swung in rhythm as the fuzzy burro marched effort-lessly up the wooded hill to the crest. Thank goodness, Gus thought, because Benny wasn't the most cooperative donkey. Sometimes he could be a real ass. If Benny decided he wasn't in the mood for something he'd stop—freeze up completely—and there wasn't a thing Gus could do to persuade him. Some people used whips or spurs or even a hot shot to make stubborn animals obey. But not Gus. Not ever.

He switched his headlamp off to save battery life.

The sound of Benny stomping through the forest along with the crisp night air seemed to ease some of Gus's suffering.

"I'll kill him…if he hurts Miss Mo…I will…do it," Gus told Benny, as a mix of emotion overwhelmed him. The thought of his grandpa being his dad only confused and disgusted him the more he tried to untangle the whole mess. Before he knew it, tears came hot and fast, like someone had turned on the spigot, and he wished he didn't care who his biological father was. It didn't matter. He had a father—a dad, and he was a good one. Will Dunnigan, the sick bastard, could go straight to hell. In fact, he was probably already there.

"Go...to hell." Gus could not quiet the tormenting truth. Snot wetted his lips while Benny stopped and waited as his rider sobbed.

He used the sleeve of his coat to dry his face and wipe his eyes. He wished Miss Mo were there to offer her wisdom, that always eased his pain. One of her best sayings had stuck with him like good poetry.

"There's pain that uses you, then there's pain that you can use." She'd said it more than once during the grueling Gloria sessions and explained that complex emotional pain from a breakup typically motivates behavior. Emotional pain is as real as physical pain. It all hurts the same but can sometimes force triumphs.

"Use the pain." He would do it for Miss Mo. Slowly, he stopped crying. Anger put a chokehold on his sorrows and he made kissing sounds to Benny, "Let's go, boy." Benny thought about it for a minute. "Come on...please. Miss...Mo's waiting." Gus reached around behind him and scratched Benny's rump. The burro twisted his head and stiffed his upper lip whenever Gus found the right spot. He scratched a bit longer. "That's all. Now...go." Benny agreed and proceeded.

"Use...the pain. Yes. Use it!" He pumped his fist and followed Forest Creek as it grew faster and louder. The sound of rushing water seemed garbled and the stars somehow distorted. Gus's head ached and his eyes got heavy. Exhaustion had snuck up on him. He'd been worried and upset and hiking for hours in the cold and definitely hadn't drunk enough water. Rushing from camp, he'd forgotten to refill the water in his CamelBak.

Gus slid off Benny and knelt next to the creek. He pushed up his sleeves, cupped his hands and dipped them into the icy water. The cold stung as he brought the water to his mouth and slurped, then repeated the process twice more, hoping his headache would subside. Gus splashed water over his swollen eyes and filled his CamelBak. He needed motivation to get going and stood up straight, raised his arms over his head, and stretched before finding a rock to boost him back on Benny.

They followed the creek about a mile give or take. Keeping track of time became impossible as Gus's mind drifted back and forth with the wind. He thought of Em. Was his young mother watching, keeping track of him from heaven? Probably, he decided, but wished he had his Magic 8 Ball to be sure. Her face from the pictures Grammy Kate had sent came to mind and shot him full of a familiar warmth he knew was love. He didn't understand how he could love someone he'd never met, but he knew it just the same.

"I will…do this for…you."

They crossed the moonlit creek, Benny's short legs hurrying and splashing water on Gus's pants because donkeys hate being wet.

"Good boy, Ben." Gus patted Benny's neck, grateful he'd gone willingly into the creek. The white underbelly of a brookie floated upside down past them and by the time they reached the cut bank two more dead fish went by. Gus pulled his glasses out of his jacket and put them on. Then, he slid off Benny and reached down into the water. He scooped and scooped the icy water until he had the stiff fish in his hand. He turned his headlamp on and inspected it closer. The fish was hard and there were no signs of trauma. Gus tossed him alongside a fallen cedar and led Benny up the creek bank—scanning the shore as he went. Clouds darkened the moon.

Around the bend the creek flattened out and a line of black plastic pipe ran from the creek. Gus followed the pipe as it snaked its way through a soggy meadow. Something white clung to a section of deer bush just across the meadow. His first thought was of Miss Mo. He dropped Benny's lead rope and ripped off the headlamp—aiming the light as he ran.

"Miss Mo." His boots sticking in the mud and the muck with every stride. Benny followed.

"Miss Mo!" He stopped. The light exposed a large piece of white plastic flapping like a trapped bird and sent Benny running back toward the creek. Gus grabbed and pulled the plastic. A bag.

"Dang it." He freed the bag and caught sight of the word *CARBOFURAN* in bold red letters. Gus knew the pesticide was toxic and had been banned from use in the US since 2009 because his dad's friend Red had been cited by the Calaveras County Environmental Management Agency for having just a few bags of the stuff on his property. The fine cost Red over three thousand dollars and he had to go to court.

These bad guys were not only hurting innocent people like Miss Mo and nice dogs like Walter, they were polluting the place he loved most. And he'd drunk the toxic water.

"Assholes. That's it!" Another reason to rid the world of bad guys. "You're…going down!" Gus snugged his headlamp over his hat and stomped off to retrieve Benny.

They rode west back across the meadow until he located the black water pipe running downhill from the creek and followed it through a maze of willow bushes. He knew he was closing in and would find Miss Mo sooner or later. He'd find her and she'd be okay. Probably scared and sad because of Walter, but when she found out Walter was alive and fed and sleeping in his teepee with Grammy Kate, she would be so happy she might cry and Gus would say *Sometimes it helps to cry and you shouldn't feel embarrassed*, like she'd said to him so many times. Hopefully, the words wouldn't stick on his tongue. Hopefully they would come out exactly how they did in his head. Hopefully, he would be a big hero this time and kill some bad guys.

But the bad guys had guns and the thought of being shot thrummed in his skull. He wondered if it would hurt—being shot.

"Of course." Idiot. But how bad would it hurt? In Westerns, being gut shot was the worst, and he hoped if someone did shoot him it would be in a place that would not make for a long, miserable death. He considered being shot in the head. The bullet would explode in his brain. That seemed terrible. And the face was even worse. Maybe the heart was best, like when you're hunting. He nodded his head. Yes. That's the place. The heart, he decided would be best. Quick and hopefully the least painful.

Dying would mean he would go to heaven and meet his mother. He could tell her about—no, show her—his orphaned buffalo, Eeyore. The thought of hugging Eeyore again brought a smile. He swatted twigs of yellow willow brush out of his face and tugged on Benny as he wondered if they let you eat hot dogs in heaven.

A terrible yowl broke the fantasy.

Gus and Benny froze and listened. Silence lasted too long, so he moved forward until it came again. Louder and longer this time. A bawling that Gus knew was a cow. Something had her stirred up because her moo was at a higher pitch, almost like bleating. It sent chills up the back of Gus's head and sent Benny braying in the opposite direction. Gus unzipped his fanny pack and pulled out his gun. With his thumb, he clicked off the safety and readied it in his right hand.

Chapter Thirteen

The long crack of gunfire bounced off the canyon walls and forced me to the precipice. Moonlight and my good eye allowed a brief assessment of an escape down the craggy granite. Calculating the best route down would have taken time and preferably daylight—luxuries I did not have. As far as I could tell this was at the very least a Class 4 descent and would have been challenging to rappel with a rope, harness, and a helmet. I couldn't recall the decimal system used in the Lake Tahoe climbing class I'd taken and it was ridiculous that it even came to mind since it made zero difference now. What I did recall was that descents were typically the riskiest. Rocks could easily become dislodged and equal disaster for even the most experienced climbers, which I was not.

"Run bitch!" Lupe's scream pushed me over the edge.

"Where you gonna go? Huh?" She was closing in on me fast by the sound of her voice.

The instinct to place the knife handle in my mouth came from out of nowhere. My teeth clamped on the bone handle as I quickly wrapped and then tied my pants around my waist. The first foot placement was always the riskiest. Turning my back on the certain death waiting below sent every nerve and muscle fiber firing. It went against my inexplicable extreme fear of heights. Just watching the documentary *Free Solo* as Alex Honnold climbed the monolithic El Capitan. The guy hung three thousand feet off the ground by his fingertips without a safety rope. The film caused a physical reaction in me. My heart rate and blood pressure skyrocketed and my palms filled with sweat. I was never interested in pursuing the skills necessary to become a real climber. The community college climbing class was simply a way to examine the benefits of conquering my deepest fears. It also became a favorite chapter in my manuscript. *You have to commit,* I recalled Sarah, my climbing instructor, saying as she hung below me at the start of my first climb.

I would have given anything to be back in that class, overlooking Lake Tahoe, shaking with a mix of fear and adrenaline but not fighting for my life. I dropped onto my stomach, faced the wall, and lowered myself. My left foot groped back and forth, stretching my toes as far down as I could. Reaching for the feel of something solid—anything before committing.

My left big toe found a bulge and I worked myself over inch by inch until it felt solid. I pressed and tested the foundation to be certain. Farther to my left a narrow lip offered the start I needed and I wedged my socked toes in as far as they would go. Stopping at the balls of both feet and gripping.

The breath I hadn't realized I'd been holding released as I forced my chest against cold wet granite. Every muscle straining against the stone in a pathetic, helpless intimacy. I looked down. The only option was farther to my left. A small crevice that I hoped would allow me room to slip my hand into and secure the next move. My grip was weakening and my calves were on fire.

The reach was more than I'd expected and my right foot fell from its perch. "Oh, God!" I didn't mean to scream as I hung in purgatory. It came up and out before I had time to reconsider or stop it. The knife fell from my mouth and banged into the darkness below.

"No. No, no, no," I whined, wishing I had a clue what to do next.

With my right hand free, I slapped it against the wall and dug for something, anything offering a lifesaving grip. "God help me. Please." I begged, then bargained, "Please, I'm sorry. Forgive me. I'll do anything." Atonement for rejecting religion and cursing God since the age of twelve hit me like lightening. Was He or She really the forgiving God the Bible promised? It seemed when facing death, one does find religion. At least I did as I committed to the move and missed the crevice completely.

My fingers slid, then found a stunted pine sapling and clamped down tight around it. The flimsy tree and I clung to life on the side of the cliff. My feet dangled midair as time slowed and seemed to stop. Below me, dark green treetops like the stained loops in the shag carpeting I'd grown up on. My brain failed to stay in the now, to stay on task. I closed my eyes.

"Thy will be done," I cried out as I envisioned my grip slipping, "on Earth," then falling fast, slamming through large limbs as I neared the end, "as it is in heaven." Death might not be swift, I feared, as I lay broken and dying in a pool of blood. Bones shattered and bent in abstract.

My white-knuckle grip refused to budge, but my brain's

release of excess cortisol turned toxic and intruded on my will to survive. Instead, I forced a conscious effort to visualize my success. If God chose to use this opportunity to redeem Him or Herself after failing me the last time, then so be it. If not, I would do it alone.

With the assistance of a healthy reticular activating system, I created my own reality. Forced imagined memories that confirmed a belief that I'd been on this rock face a thousand times before.

Like Wonder Woman, I hadn't any pants, and transformed into my favorite superhero. She could never die from a silly little fall. I recalled the Wonder Woman theme song and played it in my mind while forcing my right foot up. Spread eagle, I swung my leg up and around a rock that protruded like a gnarled finger. At the same time, I wedged my left foot into a divot and clung to life with the help of that scrawny pine rooted in the wall.

Light hit and blinded me. I closed my eyes and froze.

A gun blast, followed by an explosion of granite pelted down like rain.

Lupe laughed. "I see you." Another shot rang out and landed near my shoulder.

"Stop!" I shook as I screamed and looked down. "Please. I'll come up. You don't have to kill me. I can help you. Anything you need. I have money. I can pay you." My feeble attempt to bargain with the devil was met with another shot that annihilated the top of my tiny tree of life.

Lupe's flashlight sawed back and forth and allowed me a glimpse at the ground. Fifty feet, I estimated, possibly seventy-five, but definitely no more than one hundred. If I didn't make a move immediately, one of Lupe's bullets would surely find me, and I wondered what would be worse —a bullet in my back or the fall. My left foot slipped from the divot. There was no time to scrutinize the safest way down. I clung to the tree of life and tried in vain to find purchase. Fully exposed to Lupe's lethal capabilities, I looked down again. Surveyed the options to my left and then my right. Another shot and a spray of granite stung my bare legs like angry wasps.

The tips of my toes discovered the possibility of something solid to my left. I stretched. Shaking as I hung from the scrawny bent pine and contorted until both feet reached what felt like a bowling ball sized rock. Before releasing my hold on the sapling, I pressed my toes into the bulge, hoping it was solid enough to accept my weight. I chanced it and moved further left. It was the chance I needed—the perfect separation—a two-foot-wide break in the wall.

"The Chimney." I knew it well. What were the odds? More than simple coincidence. Inevitability? Or had God accepted my offer? Carl Jung believed meaningful coincidences are produced by a force he labeled as synchronicity, and could be considered glimpses into the unus mundus, or "one world." The theory is that there is an underlying order and structure to reality, a network that connects everything and everyone. Taking climbing classes was quite possibly synchronicity or simply God's will. Either way, I was grateful, because I knew exactly what to do next.

Slowing my mind was first and foremost. I returned to that warm sunny day on Chimney Rock above Lake Tahoe. It was the final climb of the class and the first time I had conquered some of my overwhelming fear and found a slight appreciation for the beauty in the climb. The aspect was known as the "chimney" and the technique was simple once I'd learned how to do it froggy style.

Navigating my way under the bulging granite, two more of Lupe's shots couldn't touch me. Sliding into the break, I wedged myself deeper—solidly into the opening. Secure, I slowly reached across and pulled off one sock, then reached into my fleece and shoved it into my sports bra. Carefully, I repeated the process with the other sock. Being barefoot would allow the friction necessary to begin my descent with the soles of my feet braced against the far side of the chimney wall. Slowly, I wiggled down until my back pressed firmly against the opposite side of the crack.

The granite fissure was smooth and it took everything I had to keep my palms and feet and back pressed in a counterforce move. One slip, one wrong move, and I would suffer a painful plunge. My body fused intimately with the rock as gravity observed us. Inch by slow inch, I scootched lower. Trembling my way down the slatted stone, yet somehow more encouraged with each increment of the descent. One body part after the other, until my bare feet landed on earth.

"Thank you!" I screamed and laughed. I was alive. Gunfire and gravity had lost. The little Japanese girl with the crooked bangs and buck teeth had won! Had cheated death and now looked up at the rock face lit by moonlight. I'd just free soloed! And survived.

"Woooo!" I howled at the moon. Threw my arms up over my head and pumped my fists for the first time in my entire life.

The thrill lasted only a moment before excruciating pain and exhaustion hit and I dropped to my knees. Shaking as adrenaline mixed with reality took me down. I folded onto my side. The grim odds of surviving the frigid night in this rugged wilderness clobbered my triumph.

Chapter Fourteen

Like stepping from one world into the next, Gus emerged from the thicket of willow brush and entered what was left of an illegal grow site. A thousand ghostlike cannabis plants left to wither and die. Rotting and no longer useful without their profitable buds. The pungent sweetness lingered in the air as Gus tromped his way through. He felt around his neck for the leather thong that hung there and found it. He pulled the crucifix to his lips and a skeleton key followed.

"Give me strength." He closed his eyes and kissed the crucifix.

Screeching moos from the mad cow turned to growls as Gus approached. A big red and white Herford lowered her head as steam blew from her nostrils with each howl. She rammed and rooted her nose into something on the ground. The bell around her neck jingled like a brazen alarm.

Gus shoved the gun into his back pocket and was adjusting his lamp when she charged him. He'd learned at an early age how to out maneuver buffalo, not an easy task since buffalo can outmaneuver a horse, but angry cattle required a different set of skills. And there, in the darkness, she had the advantage.

Gus turned—tried to run but she caught him in the hip with the knob of a horn. Thank goodness her owner had dehorned her, but the powerful move was enough to take Gus down. His glasses abandoned him along with every wisp of air in his lungs when her skull nailed him in the back. The bell jingling throughout the brutal attack.

Gus rolled over and landed a good punch to her nose— nothing more than a feeble attempt to alter his fate. She snorted, stepped back, then charged the instant Gus stood. His life had not flashed before his eyes. There was no beckoning bright light or glowing tunnel when the blow to the chest sent him and his headlamp flying backwards.

In the dark he went limp—like a ragdoll draped over the big cow's head. She bounced, then head-butted him under his jaw. A sickening crack as his teeth came together. Twice she connected under his jaw before flinging him into a crumpled heap on a bed of dead marijuana plants.

The killer cow did not retreat. She pressed and snorted and stomped herself into Gus's side. He thought about pulling his gun and shooting her in the head. But he couldn't move his arms—they were too busy blocking her blows. And anyway, he could never in a million years kill her. He'd much rather take the beating.

He lay there, balled up—struggling to suck in the tiniest breath, almost like he'd forgotten how, until she'd had all she wanted of him and left. The cow bell chiming the end of the match as she moseyed away the winner. That bell banged in Gus's ears for what seemed like forever. Some hero. Taken out by a mad mama cow. He'd never be able to save Miss Mo. The fact that he just didn't have hero qualities sunk in. Maybe he'd just spend the night right there, under the bright moon, curled up on a soft bed of marijuana and mud.

His tongue probed the ragged flesh inside his cheek. He tasted blood and closed his eyes as disappointment morphed into defeat and festered. Soon a long list of failures reared in his mind and tangled his thoughts. With brutal clarity, he recalled how he'd failed to rescue Gloria and she'd dumped him because of it. He'd failed to keep Eeyore safe from hunters. He'd failed to save the ranch from foreclosure. He'd failed to find his dad a good doctor who could save him, and he'd failed to keep his mom from living in a tweaker-infested trailer park. Failing Miss Mo would prove it.

"I'm an…idiot. Not…a hero—not a good guy."

Tears seeped from the corners of Gus's closed eyes as the pity party raged into overtime. A strangled cry burst from the back of his throat. What would Miss Mo think? Gus wondered. What would Grammy Kate think? Then worst of all, what would both of his moms think? One struggling to survive the trailer park and the other watching him this very moment from above. That was it. All he had to do was get up. Even the toughest hero struggled in every superhero movie he'd seen. Spiderman and Batman always seemed beaten before they found their strength and got up! All he had to do was get up.

"Get up…damn it!"

Something warm and wet touched his cheek. Gus opened his eyes and raised his fists preparing for round two.

"Benny." Gus cradled Benny in his hands and kissed his nose. "Where were you when…that cow…tried to kill me, huh?" He rubbed between Benny's eyes. "Could a used a… little help."

Gus sat up. Breathing was hard and his chest hurt really, really bad. Then he remembered, there's pain that uses you —then there's pain that you use. Benny stepped back.

A trickle of blood ran from Gus's nose and down the back of his throat. He swiped his palm across his lips and looked down at his hand in the moonlight. Dark coated his hand and he wiped it on his pants. Light gleamed twenty feet to his left.

Gus spit, wiped his face with his sleeve, and crawled to his headlamp. He knocked clumps of mud off the protective plastic and used the headlamp to scan his surroundings for the killer cow. That's when he saw it. Suddenly, it all made perfect sense.

He strapped the headlamp on and got to his knees. Before attempting to stand he reached for the gun in his back pocket. Gone. Shit. He forced a leg out and planted his foot firmly in front of him. Then made his move. Standing had never taken so much effort or will power. But he did it.

"Yes!" Pain stabbed his side, his back, and his jaw. He wrapped his arms around himself, bent over, thought about laying back down, then pictured his dad watching from heaven. His only son acting like such a crybaby over a cow. He took a step. Then another.

Benny stayed put and watched. A branch just perfect for whacking the mad cow if she returned lay in front of him and he moaned, "Owww," as he bent to pick it up.

With the stick as protection, he moved until he was close enough to see that the calf was dead. Gus shined his light on the carcass. A red and white Hereford just like his mama. He would have weighed in at around six hundred pounds but the hindquarters had been sectioned from the ribs back. Loins and rounds were gone—cuts were clean. The only animals with the ability to take down a calf this size in the forest were mountain lions or humans and mountain lions didn't remove hindquarters with such precision. Lions tended to eat through the rib cage and gorge on organs, like the heart, liver, and lungs, first. When they're done, they'll cover their kill with leaves, dirt, and pine needles. This was no lion. This was the work of a no-good poaching pot-growing animal.

Gus had to find his gun and his glasses before he could rescue Miss Mo. A stick would not be enough to kill bad guys. He looked around, trying to recall the exact spot the attack began, and hoped the mad cow would not come back. With the headlamp in his hand, he leaned on Benny. Together they scanned the ground—moving slowly in a small circle then widening a little with each step. A spiral search pattern was best for finding items and evidence, Gus had learned in his search and rescue training.

After what seemed like forever, Gus found his glasses. One of the lenses was cracked vertically right down the middle. He took a moment and thought about the gun. It could have gotten covered with dirt and he might never find it. Then what? Serves him right, he thought. He never should have shoved a gun in his back pocket. That was double dumb. He should have put it in his coat pocket and zipped it up. Better yet, a holster with a safety snap. Gus even had one, but it rubbed the skin above his hip raw and he stopped wearing it after one day.

He sighed and began a side-to-side pattern, sweeping light back and forth a foot in front of him as he went. Millions of dead marijuana leaves littered the ground and every now and then muddy little nuggets. Remnants that had broken loose from buds. Gus picked them up and stashed them in his fanny pack.

Getting high was not fun for him. Marijuana increased his anxiety and created extreme paranoia, but the CBD in the plant would help with pain if he got desperate. The nuggets needed a good washing first but the more Gus thought about it the more painful his jaw became. He reached in his fanny pack and felt around. His thumb and forefinger found a plump nugget. He blew and wiped the mud away as best he could.

"God made...dirt...and dirt...don't hurt." He popped it into his mouth, tried to chew, but it hurt too much so he forced himself to swallow. The nugget stuck and Gus gagged. Choking and coughing, he needed water. On instinct he reached for his hydration hose and gulped down the cold water before recalling the dead fish. The water in his pack was filled with toxic water and he'd just drunk more.

"Stupid!"

Gus kicked a wilting plant and set free a pain that ran up his rib cage like the time he'd held onto the hot wire fence. Electricity jolted and stung him so hard he couldn't release the wire until his dad pushed him with the plastic manure fork. He wished his dad were here. He always knew what to do under any circumstance.

Gus touched his hand to his jaw, but it didn't stop the hurt. After a few painful breaths Gus resumed his search and thought about his dad. If his biological mother and his dad were up in heaven, had they met yet? He hoped so—then the terrible idea of his biological father being there too made him stop in his tracks. Would his real dad beat up his rotten biological father?

No way heaven would have someone as bad as Will Dunnigan. He went straight to hell the minute he died. Gus resumed his search and after what his dad would have called forever and a day, he came upon the gun.

"Thank you, God. Thank you." He reached down and held the cold steel like a baby bird in his hand, then flipped the safety on. The gun stayed put in his right hand as he and Benny crossed what was left of the grow.

Chapter Fifteen

Panting, I rolled onto my back and gazed up at the full moon. The magic that I'd experienced the first time I'd slept under a full moon had waned. Stars had died, but gratitude from simply being alive and no longer shivering consoled me momentarily. The exertion had warmed me inside and out and I wanted nothing more than to stay right there and wait to rescued. I'd done my part.

But Lupe and quite possibly the man were likely hunting me. Lupe knew my exact location and odds were she knew the area, along with a much safer trek down. If I stayed put and waited to be rescued, I'd be the stereotypical sitting duck.

A rock the size of a bowling ball landed about one foot to my right. I looked up. The unmistakable clunk, clunk, of a large rock careening my way forced my hands and arms over my head. A boulder shaped like a headstone missed me by a foot. I crawled back to the bottom of the wall and tucked half myself under a mound of granite as fast as I could. A half dozen or so smaller rocks touched down. Lupe was not only relentless, she was resourceful.

"You gonna wish I got you when you're freezing to death tonight," Lupe yelled from above, her laughter slowly fading. I waited for more killer stones to roll down the cliffside, but none came. I sat up. Lupe must have found her partner by now and was busy attending to him.

Do not press the panic button yet, my mind whispered. Prioritize, I thought. What would kill me first? Being sweaty in a cold climate could and probably would cause me to become hypothermic as my body lost heat. The overnight low temperature had been averaging forty-two degrees and now that I was damp with sweat, I was at risk. Implementing cold water immersion into my daily routine might stave off some of the unwanted effects of exposure to cold, but certainly would not stop it.

"One thing at a time." I untied my pants from my waist. "One move at a time." Something warm and wet ran into my eye and down my cheek. I wiped my eye. In the moonlight, blood shined on my fingers. "Shoot." My head wound was bleeding. I must have opened the gash somehow.

Debating whether to use my pants to keep warm or stop the bleeding was the current dilemma. Adrenaline had not deterred the fact that I still had to pee badly. I could use the urine to sterilize the wound by cupping my hand and splashing what I could into it. It was gross, but I'd do it if necessary.

But that fact was fiction, I recalled. Urine is not sterile even before it comes out and gets contaminated by skin. Bacteria are always present at low levels. The stabbing pain in my head was relentless as I pulled down my underpants and crouched to urinate. That's when I noticed the wet. My underpants were soaking wet. Apparently, extreme terror accompanied by a full bladder had caused me to wet myself. My limbic system had become so intensely stressed that my brainstem could not follow my frontal lobe's commands.

I worked my wet undies off and pulled my pants on. Never had I ever gone commando. I took a quick series of shallow breaths and removed my hoodie, then my tank top. The chill in the air scratched at me but I forced it away as I worked my sports bra up and around my head wound. My socks fell. I'd forgotten I'd tucked them inside my bra. Slowly, I adjusted the bra band over the wound and the pressure seemed to work perfectly. Kate would get a good laugh if she saw me now. Carefully, I replaced my tank top, followed by my hoodie.

Debating whether to leave my underwear as a clue to my whereabouts took much too long and caused much too much confusion. Finally, I shoved the wet panties into the pouch of my hoodie.

Finding Forest Creek and moving downstream was the best option, I decided, but without shoes it would be difficult if not impossible. I had no real skills in outdoor survival and would have to improvise if I was going to survive the night. "What next?" I wrap my arms around myself and think. "You can do this. Believe it or die." I close my eyes and watch myself as if I'm the main character in an episode of Alone or better yet a documentary about my survival.

The narration begins. "She needed protection for her feet. Something soft." I looked around. Leaves or grass would work, but better yet was the—"Thick green moss that clung to the limestone behind me." I buried what was left of my nails deep between the rock and moss and stripped off hunks until I had a decent sized pile. Like I'd stuffed Joey and Patrick's Christmas stockings with goodies last year, "I stuffed moss deep into my socks."

"Necessity is the mother of invention." Packing the moss into bottom of my socks was brilliant, until I stood.

Water from the plant soaked my feet and socks instantly. That would not help my body temperature, but at least I could walk. "Body heat is lost through your head," My mother insisted every time I left the house without a beanie. Rather than argue, I wore my red wool cap until I reached the end of the block and could hide it in my coat. "My mother was wrong. People do not lose half of their body heat through their heads."

An article in the *British Medical Journal* proved that was a myth, that—"Only seven to ten percent of body heat is lost through the head." When I informed my mother of this fact, the incorrigible woman rolled her eyes and laughed. *"Words, words, words. Mean nothing. Warm head mean something."*

I adjusted the bra on my head and took a few steps. The mossy socks worked well on the uneven terrain. The recent rain had helped soften the ground under the pine needles and clumps of grass as I wandered downhill. "Every step was an effort." The numbness in my feet helped alleviate some of the pain until the stab of one spiky little pinecone, or a sharp rock, or stick, made me wish for shoes. "I will never fail to properly appreciate the invention of shoes." Then I wondered about the invention of shoes. It was a subject I knew absolutely nothing about and made a mental note to research the history of shoes as soon as I got back to my office.

There were always a vast supply of walking sticks lying around unless of course you actually needed one to survive. "Nothing was ever easy." I hunted and searched for a decent walking stick. I'd find one soon enough, I assured myself, and kept going, slow as a zombie with a bra on her head.

"Besides a walking stick, I need to keep warm." I

focused my breath the same way I'd done for the last month all because I'd been obsessed with Wim Hof—the Iceman—and his methods. I'd watched all of his videos, read his books, downloaded the app to track my daily practice. It was as if I'd found the missing link—the secret connection between mind and body. "The ancient Japanese practice of *misogi* is a similar concept of cold-water therapy done under the extremes of an icy waterfall meant to cleanse accumulated defilements and reestablish harmony in one's life."

I'd happened upon The Iceman while searching the internet for a new way on how survivors of suicide could cope with the constant guilt. Before becoming the guru he is today, Wim Hof lost his wife to suicide, leaving him and their four small children alone. The loss sent him into a deep depression and eventually on a quest to clear his mind of negative thoughts. Submerging himself in frigid temperatures, he found what he believed was the meaning to his existence. Due to his extraordinary feats, like holding the world record for being submerged in an ice bath at one hour and fifty-three minutes, the scientific community had taken note, as did I.

Forcing that wedge between the hippocampus and the nerve endings that allowed me to shiver had never been this challenging. "Shivering will warm my core temperature but only temporarily and it will deplete my fuel." My body required fuel so I simply refused to be cold. Refused to shiver.

I was scared more than I ever thought was humanly possible, but like I'd told the fish, "In spite of what you might think, you can't be scared to death." The moment I allowed doubt to infiltrate my mind I was as good as dead. "I wonder what time it is?"

"Maybe I'm closer than I think to surviving the night?" I

walked and sang "Walkin' After Midnight," by Patsy Cline. Thought it was fitting and filled my mind with memories of Kate to avoid the stress of the obvious. "Kate introduced me to the singer who'd died tragically." Her voice was unbelievably strong yet smooth as honey. I switched to singing "Crazy." And laughed at my ability to joke at a time like this. "Something a little more encouraging. Inspirational." I looked up at the man in the moon. Watching my every move, looking down like a critical grandfather. Soon he would shake his head. If he had arms, he'd cross them. I moved on.

"Slow and steady through a minefield of pinecones." My tender feet tingled as if they'd fallen asleep. Tingling distracted from the sharp stabs as my legs weakened and quivered with each step toward a grove of fat cedars covered in fluorescent green moss. Moonshine lit the glistening boughs and the scene might have made for an impressive photo were it not part of my nightmare. Coarse bracken ferns sprouted from the pine needle carpet, twisting and twirling their tentacles with the wind. Snatching at my ankle when I get too close. "Ow!"

The pungent stench of skunk permeated the air and engulfed my one unclogged nostril. "Oh my God." Like tear gas, the lingering odor burned my eyes and throat. I stopped, swallowed, and spit the foul skunk juice from my mouth. The animal had to be close, or, at the very least it had been close when it sprayed. "A skunk sprays when it feels threatened or startled." What had threatened or startled it? Man or beast?

To my right a twig snapped. I made an abrupt left and although my life may have depended on it, I was not moving at all fast. The intense sensation that Lupe or the man was closing in engulfed me like skunk spray. They could be taking aim at my back at this very moment. The urge to run away was as impossible as the urge to fly. I knew Lupe's finger was on the trigger—about to pull. A bullet in my back. Tearing through my skin and exploding my heart. I dropped and crawled behind a cedar—its thick bark frayed and split like it had survived a thousand battles. I closed my eyes and waited to live or die.

As I hid, my body rested and at times even relaxed in the silence. After what seemed like forever, I began to doubt the killers would have been patient enough to wait me out this long. I got up and continued out of the grove of mossy cedars into an open clear-cut. Stumps grayed with age signi-fied the area had been logged years ago. The chance of finding an old logging road was reasonable and improved my spirit. With hope came determination. "Think ahead." I whispered and walked. "Make plans. Make big important plans." In five months, I would be fifty-five and after what I imagined was a long while I imagined my party.

Happy birthday to you. Happy birthday to you. Happy birthday dear Maureen. Happy birthday to you. I sang in my head just in case, but come hell or high water I would give myself a birthday bash this February.

Ever since I can remember, I'd secretly wished for a surprise party. But a person needs a husband, boyfriend, brother, sister, or friends for that sort of thing. Friends typi-cally turned to acquaintances based on my tendency to analyze their poor choices. Most men and women, except Kate, don't want people digging around in their psyche unless they're paying for it.

I'd made a conscious choice to be unsociable, not marry, date, or have children. I dedicated my life to helping people. Helping my patients—and patients are not apt to throwing surprise parties for their psychologists. Besides even if I'd had someone who cared enough to gift me with a party, who would attend? Few if any. The truth hurt and I felt that familiar lump in my throat. The stinging tingle behind my eyes and there it was. A good stick, perfect for walking! I reached down and grabbed it. It was long but if I could break it in two, I'd have a decent set. I smashed the dead limb against a madrone and it broke into four pieces. Not at all what I'd hoped for, but I had one, and one was better than none. I planted the stick and stepped with my sore feet.

"Much better." I didn't resemble such a limping zombie. Though I was still moving at a sloth's pace, my speed seemed to have increased slightly with the aid of the stick. I might cover a mile in the next two or three hours.

Walking and lost in the dark forest offered much too much time for my thoughts to take over and wander aimlessly. To question everything and dwell on every mistake I'd ever made that contributed to this very moment. I didn't feel like narrating my survival anymore because I didn't want the world to hear the truth about me. It all came down to being alone. If only I'd had a partner, it is quite conceivable that I would not be in the awful predicament.

Abraham Maslow's hierarchy of needs—the rainbow-colored triangle took up my occipital lobe and explained perfectly why I would never reach the top level of self-actualization I craved. Level three is belonging and love and includes intimate relationships and friends. My inability to connect with people outside of therapy sessions was the reason I would forever be detained from reaching self-actualization. I was consistently evaluating people and tended to keep colleagues at a distance, never accepting invitations for dinner, or parties, and especially not cocktails.

I hadn't taken a drink since college, when my drinking

caused an innocent man's death. I'd hit a homeless man who'd been crossing a dark street, but poor judgement came with being drunk and I didn't stop for one block. Felony hit-and-run. My conscience sobered up and forced me to turn around. The old man was dead next to a decomposing Oldsmobile. At three AM no one was there to help or care or convict. I drove to a payphone and called my boyfriend Patrick, who happened to be Kate's older brother. Their father was a judge and had kept me, his son's girlfriend, from being arrested, questioned, or suspected. It was a secret they'd taken to their graves. But the guilt—that would never die. I swore that if I survived the night, I would confess and willingly accept whatever punishment the law deemed fit.

Not everyone wants to look deep into the mirror, but I refused to evade the opportunity to take a good hard look at myself whenever possible. Before offering insight therapy at my clinic, I underwent six months of intensive insight therapy myself, with the head of the psychology department at Stanford University. After six months, he concluded that throughout my childhood, I lacked close relationships with relatives and peers, and thus grew into an adult who harbored negative views about connecting with others. I didn't disagree yet kept the hypnopompic hallucinations to myself. Since there is no cure nor treatment, so what would be the point?

The ground leveled out. A variety of conifers in every size and shape surrounded me as I surveyed the area. It was reasonable to question whether or not I was traveling deeper into desolation. I knew where I'd been fishing but I'd run a fair distance and had no inkling of where the man had brought me when I was unconscious. The weed camp couldn't have been too far, I assumed, because the man had probably carried me. Straight ahead felt wrong, but so did wandering aimlessly through the forest like a slack-jawed tourist. I chalked it up to gut feeling or possibly instinct.

"Wayfaring something or other." The word wayfaring triggered more than a person traveling on foot. For some reason I connected the word to society's loss of natural navigation skills. Humans have become so reliant on GPS that our instincts to find our own way have gone extinct. I was guilty. I'd allowed my own magnetic pull, my most basic navigational skills, to atrophy. Now pointing my socked feet left or right would be a life-or-death decision.

"Fuck." I'd said it. Out loud. Finally. It honestly felt good—like a slight relief. Perhaps Kate's potty mouth had rubbed off on me. "Fuuuck!" I screamed and my head ached. My face heated as frustration forced action. Dogs could find their way home from across the country. Why couldn't I feel that one direction was right and the other was wrong?

"Eeny, meeny, miny, *Mo*." I went right. Cutting along the side of a slope for the next half an hour. Dead timber and hundred-year-old stumps like skeletons and headstones as I passed through. Branches crunching now and then beneath my tender feet. The rhythmic stab of my walking stick into earth with each small stride. A second stick rested next to a stump and I snatched it up. Two walking sticks seemed to lessen some of the shaking heaviness in my weak legs, thus improving my mood. Probably placebo, but who cares. I was grateful for the effect and forced a grin which, unfortunately, sent my swollen eyeball into a frenzy of what felt like a million excruciating pinpricks. I stopped smiling and gently rubbed my eye.

Standing in silence, my stomach churned and murmured. Now hunger threw in its two cents as well.

What to consume upon my return to civilization? I plodded.

"Udon soup." The thought of slurping up the warm broth and long noodles made my stomach feel even more hollow.

With a stick in each hand, I trekked approximately another half mile.

Then a gurgling. I stopped and listened to be sure it wasn't me. In less than a second, the sound turned into a heavenly chorus. My heart accelerated and so did I. Rushing as best I could toward the sound of running water.

Chapter Sixteen

Moonlight slanted through the forest, reflecting off enthusiastic water rushing below. Forest Creek, I hoped, but couldn't be certain. It was possible that it was a fork of the Mokelumne River I knew was nearby. If it were the Mokelumne, downstream would eventually lead to civilization. But how far down, that was the question I had no answer for.

The glistening serpent in all its sinuous glory seemed to wink at me from below a twenty-foot embankment. A massive spring runoff had washed away the entire hillside above the creek. Rather than struggle hoping to finding a safe way down, I kept the creek in sight and followed it downstream from above. Nothing below looked familiar. None of it looked right, but I kept going because what option did I have?

"You can't quit now. What would John Muir think? He survived blizzards with a biscuit and a blanket, for crap's sake." We've become such a soft society. Turing up the heat when we're cold and the air when we're hot. We eat when we're hungry and even when we're not. "It is through suffering that our bodies adapt." I picked up my pace. Looked down at my dirty big toe poking through my sock and force a positive thought.

The woman—what was her name? She'd hiked the entire Pacific Crest Trail alone, with no one resupplying her. In just over two months she set a speed record of 2,650 miles. Then she turned around and hiked another 8,000 miles alone in eight months to complete the Appalachian, the Pacific Crest, and the Continental Divide Trails back to back. "She hiked through waist-deep snow and averaged twenty-five miles a day all because she wanted to." Then it hits me. "Anish!" That was it. "Her trail name was Anish." I couldn't recall her real name, but perhaps her previous identity no longer mattered.

I stopped and looked back at the distance I'd come while occupying my mind with inspiring trivia. At least the equivalent of one city block. "You go Mo." I'd become my own patient, offering the same encouragement I'd offer any suffering human.

A territorial fox screamed in the distance. A constant gekkering—guttural   ack-ack-ack-awooo-ack-ack-ack. Followed by the occasional yelp. A second fox didn't take the threat lightly and howled back. *Surviving With Wolves*: the Misha Defonseca story popped into my mind.

It was and still is my favorite memoir, about a young girl who'd survived the Holocaust by hiding out in the wilderness and eventually being raised by a pack of wolves. The book was so inspiring that I bought copies for nearly everyone I knew, including some of my patients. It was later revealed that the author had written an audacious deception to hide an even darker truth. The publisher sued and readers were outraged. I, on the other hand, considered how the story had impacted readers and inspired them to push past their trauma. That was the important story despite fabrications from the author.

Two foxes yipped in unison.

"Maureen and the Foxes." I snickered, then forced a laugh. "Hilarious. Very witty. Clever, given the situation. Quite possibly brilliant." Ahead, the ground grew higher and higher away from the creek. I regretted not taking the twenty-foot embankment when I had the chance. I limped along. Maybe I should turn around and backtrack right now. Not one more lame step. I could hardly see the creek below, but I could hear it and kept going.

"This has to be it. Downstream."

Cold crept in and I fought off the shivers as long as I could. "Shivering burns up fuel. Once you start, you cannot stop," I reminded myself for the second time tonight. One slow step at a time, I climbed until the creek was completely out of sight. I was much too high, but the echo of rushing water rose from below, proving it was still down there somewhere in the dark, waiting to show me the way home. My teeth chattered as I shivered.

Like a dying salmon swimming upstream, I weaved my way around rocks, over dead and dying timber, and through brush I hoped was not poison oak. Uphill, tapping the ground in manic rhythm with my walking sticks. Growing weaker with every step until it was as if I was trying to move through thick mud.

My mind smothered in a wooly fog. All I wanted to do was lie down, close my eyes, and sleep. Exhaustion and cold had sunk its fangs in deep and would not let go. I forced a step and then another followed by another until suddenly the terrain shifted—shedding its evergreens and turning to stone. I stopped atop a long section of scarred and raged granite dangerously sloped and wet. A narrow slice of creek prowled forty or fifty feet below. The steep slab appeared to be at least one hundred feet across. Above me, sheer wall that refracted the sound of turbulence.

Disoriented, I closed my eyes and concentrated. Searching for a feeling—the Force. Direction. "I'm so lost." I finally admitted it. Being lost isn't the worst thing that can happen. Maybe it was best to stop here, stay put, and wait for help.

"They'll find me." I sat, shivering uncontrollably on top of the slick rock, so smooth it was as if Mother Nature herself had sanded it over eons. A numbness took over and I failed to feel the cold on my buttocks or the chill from the wind funneling up the narrow canyon. "They *will* find me." I doubted anyone but Kate would search for me, especially at night. "Who cares enough to come out here in the middle of the night in the cold and the rain?" I laughed to avoid crying.

I couldn't help but let regret bleed out. On that damp granite, lost in space and time, my mournful lament harmonized with the wind in the trees and the blathering creek beneath. One painful memory led to another and finally landed on the agonizing loss of my mother to a drunk driver. Synchronicity for what I'd done, the life I took, years ago.

I'd confessed the entire ugly truth about my drinking one winter evening after Kate had insisted I try her home-made hard cider. Kate seldom lacked gritty enlightenment, but for once she was speechless when I confessed that I'd hit and killed a homeless man and that the judge that kept me from prosecution was her father. I sat in silence as Kate poured the entire batch of cider down the drain. She'd spent days pressing apples. Months fermenting and adding sugar to the gallon bottles. Grating fresh cinnamon sticks. "That is completely unnecessary, Kate," I'd said as she dumped a second gallon down the drain.

"You're right. Alcohol is now completely unnecessary in our home." Kate hugged me with more love and compassion than I'd felt in my entire life. I only wished I'd been brave enough to tell her the truth. At the time, I wasn't willing to jeopardize losing my best friend by confessing that I'd fallen head over heels in love with her. Instead, I moved out.

Sorrow ran its course until utter despair took over. Tears turned cold on my face—surprising how many I'd stored over the years. Even the eye that was swollen so tightly shut sprang a leak. I threw my walking sticks out in front of me. They banged and slid away like spears into emptiness. Never signifying when or if they hit water. I let myself down, curled into a fetal position, and brought my knees to my chest. Shivering with my arms wrapped tightly around my knees, I sobbed and sobbed until rain tapped my shoulder.

I sat up. Adjusted the sports bra away from my forehead and considered my options. I could not and would not stay here and suffer a miserable death. Going up was not an option even if I had climbing gear and a helmet. Down would be a terrifying slide to a watery grave. Forward or back were the only options and there was nothing to be gained by going back other than death by Lupe.

"Forward." I crawled. Slowly. On my hands and knees. Carefully, across the slope. My attempt was courageous but futile. Instantly I slid. Downward. The smooth wet granite and incline had the advantage. Trees seemed to float higher and higher, but I was the one moving. Flat out, sliding on my stomach and gaining speed. I clawed at anything and everything with my hands and feet. Fighting to stop the friction burning my thighs. Wet moss filled my hands, but failed to stop or even slow me down. I careened toward the creek.

The slope lessened toward the bottom and the sliding slowed so much so that I'd likely stop before plunging into the water. I clung and heaved a euphoric sigh of relief into the wall. My body intimately pressed against the stone as I slipped in slow motion. There I was on the face of the gray wall under the moon, barely moving, but moving just the same. Unable to stop. The rush of water reaching out and tugging me, refusing to let up until it had me. A surprisingly quiet splash and I was gone.

Chapter Seventeen

The farmhouse broke into three pieces, then floated away. Waves burst through the windows and flooded the living room as Kate shoved Patrick, then Joey, out of the water and onto the floating sofa. The boys quickly drifted away on their sofa lifeboat out into a never-ending ocean of turbulence. Kate swam as hard and fast as she could, but never progressed in the cruel current. The roof cracked and caved with an avalanche of white. She kicked and fought as the entire room tumbled. Sorrow weighed her down. She sank. Deeper and deeper.

With her last breath, she released a lifelong lament, and surrendered. Drowning alone in the dark abyss, she wept until the tug. A big silver hook pierced her ear. Pulling her slowly at first, then faster up toward the truth. The surface was bright, clear, and wonderfully calm. Joy filled her lungs as she breathed in and saw the strongest, bravest, smartest person she knew reeling her in. Floating on the kitchen table, Mo set her rod down and reached her hand out to

Kate. The boys and Gus sat cross-legged alongside her, eating hot dogs on sticks while Walter barked.

She woke like a woman drowning in black water, gasping but not desperate for air. For something more. Something as real as the dream that had just unfurled destiny like a mural. A truer, more meaningful vision of what life could be hung within her reach. Love rippled through her and she sat up. Most people find someone and gradually fall in love, never knowing exactly when it happened—but Kate knew. She recognized it the second it happened. All the feelings she'd been holding back came flooding in at that precise moment. She loved Mo. With all her heart, she loved the woman. It had taken the possibility of losing her forever to stop looking at what was in front of her and see what was inside. There was no going back. If given the chance, the first thing she'd do was tell Mo just how much she loved her and how sorry she was for not recognizing it sooner.

Walter sat up next to Kate, barking, as a cough rumbled from deep in her chest. With just enough light to see, she found a bottle of water on the stump and gulped half of it down before realizing the fire was out and she was cold. Damn cold. Mo would go around the house opening windows whenever Kate was trying to heat it up. Kate believed seventy-five was a reasonable room temperature, while Mo insisted they stop living in a cocoon of comfort and keep the house no higher than sixty-five. She even went so far as to print out study after study proving a never-ending summer is detrimental to metabolic health, and left them stacked on the kitchen table under Kate's morning coffee. Kate had used the paper to start a fire in the woodstove while Mo shook her head, rolled her eyes, and smiled. That smile. The way her upper lip pulled tight across her teeth. She was beautiful if you took the time to really look.

Pain and cold and a whole lot of regret clamped down on her chest. Along with the cough, Kate wished she could hack up and spit out her mistakes with the viscous mucus.

"Gus?" She stood and approached the firepit. Walter raised his head, his sap-bandaged ear hanging heavy to one side as he watched her. With a stick, she stirred the coals and added wood.

"Gus." How long had she been asleep? Couldn't have been more than fifteen or twenty minutes, Kate guessed. She pulled her flip phone out of her coat pocket and checked the time.

"Holy shit." It was almost eleven o'clock. She'd slept three hours and was still tired. Seldom, if ever, did Kate feel this completely knackered. Only when she was sick.

Had she caught the dreaded virus somehow? She'd been socially distancing most of her life—it wasn't even a thing for her. Only places she ever went were the post office and the grocery. She wore her mask, washed her hands, but Ed was meeting daily with clients in the county jail where there'd recently been an outbreak. He wasn't ill as far as she knew. Maybe it was just old age and running around the forest worried sick about Mo had caught up with her.

Where the hell was Gus?

"Gus!" Yelling sent Kate's cough into a frenzy. Her thoughts immediately went to a worst-case scenario. The guy with the gun got him, she feared. He had taken or killed sweet Gus and she was next.

"Motherfuckers." It all came rushing back. The radio dispatch from Danny K. Where the hell were they? That was three hours ago. Something was definitely not right. They should have been here by now. What time had they heard from Danny K.? A bit after eight, she thought, and rubbed her eyes.

Maybe they'd found her. Why had she assumed the worse? They must have found her. That made the most sense. Odds were, they'd found her that's why no one had arrived yet. Yes. A sense of relief filled Kate until she continued to think. Dear God, was she dead or alive? Kate's heart hurt and suddenly she felt more helpless than ever. She wasn't even sure where the hell she was or how to get home from Gus's camp on her own. Especially in the dark. Dawn could not come soon enough.

Walter growled and leaped to the entrance. His blond hair bristled along his back as Kate followed. There on the canvas wall alongside the flap were the words.

B BACK SOON
U STAY HERE!

Written in charcoal at eye level. He'd even used an exclamation mark and that eased Kate's fear. She grinned thinking of him writing the note as she slept. Such a bossy little man.

Her head told her Gus was right. She should stay put, but her heart told her she should do something more. At the very least, put forth every effort to save Mo. Staying there wouldn't help Mo one damn bit. If Kate really wanted to find her, she wouldn't sit around the fire drinking cocoa waiting for Mo to come strolling in.

Walter barked and nosed his way out through the door flap. Kate rushed to the bedroll—found her headlamp and pulled the gun from her coat pocket. Outside, she scanned the dark with the light in one hand and her .38 revolver in the other. Cold air stung her lungs.

"Gus, you out here?" She listened. "This ain't the time to be messin' around." Walter barked near the creek. Kate moved slowly and cautiously toward him as sticks broke like brittle bones underfoot. She worked her light and strained her eyes to adjust. At the creek, there was an edge to the darkness. The air carried a nervous tension as Walter snarled.

Splashing and the clunk of rocks tumbling against each other came from the creek. Kate aimed her light toward the sound, but she didn't need a headlamp to recognize the mass of cinnamon-colored fur molesting the ice chest.

The sow had to have weighed close to five hundred pounds as she rocked back on her haunches. Her height grew like a furry bush planted in the water. She lifted her wet snout and sniffed the air as her paws dangled at her sides. Suddenly, the bear huffed and woofed. Walter quit barking the instant she dropped onto all fours and began swinging her head back and forth. Kate had dealt with plenty of bears over the years, but this one was a monster and her warning was not to be taken lightly. This was her jackpot, stay away or else. She flipped the ice chest and pounced on it. Over and over.

"Get!" Kate put her headlamp on, picked up a rock, and pitched it as hard as she could at the sow. It flew over her head and ker-plunked behind her. She didn't even bother turning to look, just clawed and bit the corners of the ice chest.

"Get! Go on!" Kate screamed. "Get outta here!"

The sow slapped the ice chest into deeper water. It floated away and she pounced like a kitten when it sunk. It popped up, caught in the current, and picked up speed. The wet bear loped down the creek, her red fur undulating as she went, until the bear and the ice chest disappeared around the bend.

Walter returned defeated, and looked at Kate. She

thought about following the bear. Firing a shot and trying to spook it away. Feeding bears is one of the worst things a person can do to a bear and Kate knew it. A fed bear is a dead bear.

"I can't save the entire fucking world," she told Walter. "Can't even save Mo."

On the way back to the teepee, Kate looked for Benny. He wasn't at his shelter and she wondered if he was just off grazing or if Gus had taken him. Burros are like big-eared alarms. Soon as they hear or sense any sort of danger, they bray. At least the two that Kate owned did. Odds were good that Gus had taken him or he'd have been hee-hawing a warning with a bear that close to camp.

As she neared the teepee, the grumble of a motor approached.

"Holy shit," Kate whispered. Was it the sheriff's department, finally? Search and Rescue coming to fill her heart with love or shred it to pieces? A light bounced toward Kate from her left. She started toward it, then thought better of it and stopped. She turned off her headlamp. Maybe it wasn't one of the good guys. Maybe, as Gus had put it, one of the bad guys was approaching. Kate couldn't be sure and took cover behind a big cedar. She waited. Walter followed, then stood nearby wagging his tail—announcing her hiding place to anyone interested. "Get, Walter. Go lay down," Kate ordered in a whisper.

Walter lowered his head and took a few steps back, but wouldn't quit looking at Kate. Probably wondering what she was up to. The four-wheeler pulled up to the teepee and squeaked to a stop. Kate cautiously poked her head out just far enough to watch with one eye.

Danny K. turned off the motor. "Hello, Kate. It's Dan. You in there?"

"Down here," she answered and rushed to him.

"Did you find her?" she asked.

"Oh, thank goodness. You're okay," Danny K. stammered. "No."

"No?" Kate didn't know whether to rejoice or mourn. "Shit."

"Gus radioed and said you were here and getting very sick. I came to give you a ride back to your pickup truck."

"I don't need a ride! What's going on with finding Mo, for Christ's sake?" Her irritation came through loud and clear.

"Sheriff's department will be here first thing in the morning. Also, the local search and rescue is organizing their volunteers. They should be stationed by midmorning or afternoon at the very latest."

"That's *fucking* bullshit." Kate threw her arms in the air then turned away to cough.

"Everyone's doing the best they can, Kate. Good grief, you sound terrible. Please let me take you home. There is absolutely nothing you can do to find Mo tonight other than get yourself into trouble, and then we'll be out looking for two missing people tomorrow. And to be honest, Kate, that's somewhat selfish if you think about it."

"I'm *not* going home." She looked at Walter and wished he could use his sixth sense to find his owner. "How about you drive me around and we'll search for Mo together?"

"I've been everywhere I can get to—driving around off road in the dark is too dangerous. Headquarters already ordered me to stand down. If they find out I'm even out here they could fire me."

"What is *wrong* with people?" Kate shook her head and hoped to hell the tears building behind her eyes wouldn't fall because if they did it'd be a long while before she'd get them stopped. And crying in front of anyone besides Mo wasn't something Kate did.

"*Please*, I'm begging you. Let me take you to your truck."

"No." Kate neared the teepee and stopped at the door flap. She looked back at Danny K. "Thanks for trying to help. Sorry to be so...you know—but a person I love is missing and I feel..." Kate took a deep breath, "so unbelievably useless."

"It's okay. I understand. I'm just really sorry about the entire situation. All I ask is that you do not venture out anymore tonight. Just wait until daylight and we'll figure this out together. I promise. Okay?"

Defeat stung Kate's nose and her eyes watered. She couldn't hold back any longer—couldn't speak—just nodded her compliance as Danny K. started up his four-wheeler and turned around. Kate watched him go, then stepped inside the teepee with Walter to purge her demons with a damn good cry.

Chapter Eighteen

The icy water shocked my system like a thousand needles. Raw grinding pain that possessed me like a demon, followed by a release of submerged gasps in pressurized darkness.

I opened my eye but there was nothing to see. My upside-down mind and body screamed in muted electrocution. Every nerve firing. Blood vessels slammed shut.

The current sucked me backwards faster and faster. I broke the surface. Gasped for air. My weary body flopping like a fish out of water. White noise and white water weighing me down.

Panicked kicking and ragged breaths as I fought to relax and bring my feet around in front of me, a strategy I'd learned the hard way while rafting last summer.

A class IV rapids on the North fork of the Flathead River terrified me the moment I saw it. Instantly, I'd regretted my decision to tempt death. The force of rushing water thrashed the raft and catapulted the nose. That's when I caught sight of it. The Ledge.

The rafting guide had warned us about this section. The

river disappeared and the plummet seemed unsurvivable. I closed my eyes and gripped to the safety rope with both hands as we nosedived over The Ledge. The force when we landed bounced me high enough to watch the raft leave without me.

The chaotic water punched the air from my lungs. Choked me down with its cold. "Don't fight it!" I'd heard someone somewhere scream as I sucked a mix of air and water into my lungs. Choking in the turbulence, I'd forgotten our previous safety lessons.

After the initial shock, I pushed the helmet up, away from my eyes, and forced myself to do what I'd prescribed to most of my patients. A technique known as box breathing. It helped calm my mind by distracting it while I focused on counting and breathing in. One, two, three, four, five, six, I released and counted out to six. Once more and I leaned back, brought my legs in front of me, and let the life vest do its job.

Before I knew it, I'd reached calmer water. The second raft plucked me out of the water as quickly and easily as pulling up a fish. To me it was an epochal event. The day I glimpsed the meaning of life by flirting with death.

But now, there was no life vest and my legs were uncooperative logs. I quit fighting and allowed the current to have its way with me. The weight of the water heaved me up, then stomped me down. Thrusting me faster, back and forth and up and down. The force built by the composition of the earth over thousands of years. Miles upstream and down with such a sense of purpose. It seemed to be straining to get me somewhere.

High granite walls nearly vertical narrowed in on both sides and the merciless torrent couldn't release me if it had wanted to. My back slammed into what I suspected was a rock though oddly it didn't hurt. I was too limp, or too numb, or both. The impact flung me midstream, spun my feet out in front, right where I wanted them to be. The gorge widened ahead. Stars closing in and trees leaning down like spectators with morbid curiosity.

A wash of endorphins swept through me—giving off a euphoric high as I spit water. Like a woman in labor, I focused the breath I'd practiced every day for the last month under a cold shower. The ice bath I'd planned to take on Monday had come early.

Time slowed. The world crawled by. It felt like ages. Rocks and boulders passed, protected by glass waiting to shatter under the massive moon. My bare toes poked up and out of the water swollen white and oddly unfamiliar. Where had my socks gone? I was aware of the oddity of noticing.

"You have the most beautiful feet." Kate had looked and sounded surprised when she'd said it. We had taken the twins to Schaads, a secluded little lake close to the ranch. The water was warm and we had the entire place to ourselves. Walter and the boys played fetch while Kate taught me to swim. I floated on my back and for the first time in my life I'd felt brave. Something about Kate always gave off a sense of security. As if no matter how bad the world got, she would save me.

The day was magical as Kate floated alongside me in the middle of Schaads Lake. It was one of the best days of my life, and I'd hoped it was Kate who'd locate my body. Kate. No one else would take care of the important details like a biodegradable coffin and a green burial. But who would take care of Kate? So many thoughts in so little time.

My body bogged down and my rear collided then scraped the rocky bottom. The force plowed me through the shallows. I pressed my hands along my sides and felt the grit of sand underneath, then rolled onto my stomach. Using my limbs like a million-year-old tetrapod to crawl to shore. Evolved as I fell flat just out of the water. With my forehead resting on the shore, I closed my good eye. Thoughts consisted of nothing but the oxygen entering and exiting my lungs.

Breathing through my mouth played peacefully—soothing as wind on waves. An ocean moving me in and out. My pulse accompanying the creek pushing me away. My eye opened. Sand became a billion shiny black and brown and white pebbles, like humanity standing together to hold me up. I raised my head. The moon pulled. The mountains lifted. The unity of the universe set forth an acceptance. "You can't kill me!" I laughed. "I'm already dead."

Death would occur soon enough. There was no need for fear or dread. If given the choice, I would much rather die here than beneath that foul potbellied wretch after he'd raped me. Dying is the least terrible thing that can happen to the living. The saying came like a meteor, but I could not recall if my mind had recovered it or it was the last brilliant discovery I would ever make. I'd accomplished more in the last few hours than I had in my entire life.

Pride had never been a virtue to me or maybe it was just I'd never accomplished feats to be proud of until now. I replayed my escape from the man and the attempted murder I might regret not committing. Saving future victims would have balanced the scales of good and evil. I would never have thought myself capable of descending that vertical cliff face without a rope, or staying afloat while the icy creek tried to swallow me in the middle of the night. Not in a million years. I had wasted my superhuman strengths until now. Maybe we all did, and it simply took the need to survive to awaken them. Like Misha and her literary forgery *Surviving With Wolves.*

I rolled onto my back—below a stately sugar pine. Uncontrollable shivering began with a vengeance. Above me, golden oak leaves quivered sympathetically. Pine and cedar boughs waved hello. Or was it goodbye? Under my eyelids, Kate waited for me with a warm smile that stretched out into a terrific brightness reminiscent of the morning sun.

My chattering jaw mumbled, "I love you." Lips bouncing off my teeth. I thought of Kate and the difficulties she'd have to endure surviving yet another death. And the twins. I always knew how much I truly loved Kate. And the boys too. For the life of me, I could not comprehend why I hadn't once hinted. Why hadn't I insisted, explained, or at the very least confessed? The cold realization made my pulse quicken.

"Love…"

A warmth sprouted in my heart. "I love you." And grew in my chest. I sat up and with my mud-caked fingernail I drew a heart. It was the one genuine regret I'd take to the grave.

Unrequited love. A single sparkle clung to my eyelashes and refused to fall. Then, as if it was the last thing I'd ever do, with a shaking finger, I slowly wrote after the heart—U, then K. "Love you, Kate." I spoke, but could *not* feel my lips move. Skin so cold it stung, then slowly burned. Heat spread from my head to my toes until I was on fire. I fought my wet fleece until I worked it off over my head and realized I'd lost my sports bra bandage somewhere.

I got to my hands and knees, hotter than hell, and crawled to a boulder. Allowed its solid and stoic strength to help me stand. I swayed with the forest and stepped clumsily ahead to a dying pine bent in half as if it were bowing—greeting me with respect. I clung to the broken tree. Peeled at the scabby bark until it bled. Soon it would bleed to death if I didn't save it. I pulled my shirt off and wrapped it around the trunk. It worked. The bleeding stopped. Now if only I could stop the sweltering heat burning me up from the inside out. I went to the creek and removed every stitch of clothing.

Darkness came the moment my bleeding feet stepped into Forest Creek.

"Fate." My breath clouded, reminding me I was still alive and shivering.

"Kismet." I moved primal—graceful—deeper into the urgent and complicated current. It's blathering rumbled my head like a nightmare, but all too real.

The shivering ceased.

"Destiny." Water splashed my thighs. Up my torso into a numbing heat like nothing I'd ever felt before. There was no cold left in me. Stumbling over rocks tainted with slick algae, I fell. My hands buried in the viscous bottom, face to face with the bruised and beaten stranger in the water. Staring deep into her orbs—to see what darkness hid under the surface.

"Liar," she whispered.

I crawled away from her, into the shallows as the creek rambled on—an endless rhapsody of nothing in particular, like my overdramatic patients. All of them like water, running from something in the past. I'd lost track of time and fumbled from the creek. Willingly, into the cauterized world, where trees cast bony shadows in moonlight.

The forest suffered from motley shades of black. Year-old smoke and the essence of charred remains carried a tinge of sweetness. On my hands and knees, but unable to recall the moment I'd succumbed to crawling. Slowly. My long limbs like a praying mantis stalking her lover. Ravens followed. Watching. Awaiting sunrise to pluck out my eyes should I quit. Their sharp beaks pecking holes in my flesh. Holes in my story. Past the bone, down to the marrow. To the real me before the world told me who to be.

I moved toward the improbable warmth of scorched earth until it gave way to a massive hole. A stump hole. The remains of a monstrous pine which had burned and sunk to ash. Heat like open arms drew me in and I burrowed myself deep inside the blackened den. Ashes to ashes, dust to dust. And earth as soft as a silk cocoon. In the fetal position, my soul found repose. I closed my eyes and drifted away until I saw the light.

Chapter Nineteen

Past the grow the way wasn't obvious. Gus knew the area and took the uphill approach to the camp. Growers could keep watch from their perch above. A perfect lookout. They would know if anyone, especially law enforcement, had arrived. Plants would be eradicated and growers would lose big-time money, but at least there would be an escape route in the opposite direction. This was why hardly anyone ever got busted in a National Forest marijuana raid. But Gus had to be careful. He knew the growers were armed and dangerous.

"But...so am I," Gus told himself. "Armed...and *dangerous*." The moon offered light, but Gus needed to move unseen. He slipped the headlamp off his beanie and tucked it inside his coat pocket. He adjusted his hat down over his ears.

Benny didn't want to climb and stopped after only a few steps.

"We have to. Come...on." He pulled and leaned back on Benny's lead rope and after a tug-o-war, the burro finally gave in. He followed Gus willingly up the bluff. Rocks and debris falling below them as they went. Twice, Gus stopped to catch his breath and feel the swelling in his jaw. He was probably dehydrated and needed a drink of water, but not that toxic crap he'd gotten from the creek. He wondered if it might be too late. Maybe the water he'd been drinking all summer was poisoned. Maybe he would get the sickness like his dad and soon he would die for no good reason too. The thought along with the weed jarred him into serious paranoia.

He felt sick to his stomach and thought he'd barf when they reached the rocky top. The terrain leveled into mostly granite. Gus wiped his brow with his fingertips. His heart seemed to clap in his chest. Applauding the accomplishment of getting this far. Benny kept going in a hurry for once and Gus had to trot to keep up. As they neared a fallen and dead cedar, Benny stopped. The burro lowered his head and snorted. This, Gus knew, was Benny's language for something's wrong.

Gus dropped Benny's lead rope and left it hanging as he approached the log with his gun pointed and ready. A snort sent every nerve in Gus's body running. The fear and urge to retreat and go back to his warm teepee and eat a hot dog with Walter and Grammy Kate were overwhelming.

Be brave, he told himself. Be brave. You're the good guy. These are bad guys. You got this. He forced his stiffening and sore legs forward. Past the log to his right, the bad guy sat against a massive sugar pine. The lookout on guard duty was sleeping on the job. A wool blanket wrapped around his shoulders and a San Francisco Giants cap on his head as he snored. Gus never hated anyone, but he was pretty sure he hated this guy. If his biological father were still alive, he might hate him too. But this guy was the worst of the alive bad guys.

Shoot him in his sleep. That would be the best for them both. Gus raised the gun and Benny brayed like an alarm clock. The man woke with a look of utter confusion that quickly morphed into sheer terror when he caught sight of Gus. He tried to stand.

"Don't move." The words came out strong and perfect. Just like Gus had imagined.

Homer's mouth hung open and his bushy eyebrowns puckered into one fury unibrow. It was a look of pure disbelief.

"Gus, hey. Hi. What are you doing?"

Gus held the gun with two shaking hands. "You poached...a calf...that did...not belong...to you." He stepped closer—keeping the gun leveled at Homer's chest.

"We were starving." He raised his hands. "We had to eat."

"Did...you...have to...shoot...a *dog*?" Rage clogged his words. "Did...you...have to *poison*...the creek?" Gus's face burned red hot. "You shot...Walter!"

"No. No, no," Homer pleaded. "Gus, put the gun down, man." Homer lowered his hands halfway. "You still pissed about me and Gloria?"

"No." Gus's face tightened.

"Good. Cause we're way past that shit, right?"

"You hurt...Miss Mo. She is—"

"NO! Swear to God. I saved her ass. She ate shit and—"

"You...are...a liar! You stole...her hat!" Gus closed in on Homer. He remembered Miss Mo wearing that exact hat when he ran into her fishing. The heavy gun shook in his hands. His numb arms weakening as he tightened his grip.

Homer pulled the cap off and tossed it on the ground. "Yes. I took her hat. Doesn't mean I hurt her. Fuck, dude."

"You...are a...bad guy."

Homer reached his right arm behind him. Gus knew he was armed.

"Freeze!" Gus closed his eyes and pulled the trigger, but nothing happened.

The pause set Homer in motion. He got to his feet with a silver gun in his hand while Gus's mind glitched—working out why the trigger had locked rather than reacting. He'd blown his chance. Forgotten to release the damn safety. And now Homer was up and coming at him full force with the scariest face Gus had ever seen. The hero inside him quickly decided the best thing to do was to run. A sharp penetrating shriek escaped Gus as he turned and ran for his life.

Neither man was fast. Gus wanted to slow down. Stop and just forget the whole thing, but there wasn't time. His mind seized as he raced across the rocky ridgeline. His boots slapped the granite spread out in front of him like a table and he wished he'd worn his high-top hiking boots.

He'd been there before and knew the egg-shaped rock ahead would give him the advantage. If only he could get himself up and over the rock before being shot, Homer wouldn't stand a chance. Gus could hide in the big crevice on the backside of egg rock and the minute Gloria's stupid boyfriend climbed down—BAM! Shooting from the protective cover of the crevice would be genius. The work of an intelligent hero.

Climbing egg rock with a gun in his hand was not wise, and halfway up, Gus slipped. On his elbows, sliding backwards, the gun scraped against the hard surface until he was back where he started. Gus could feel Homer closing in as he tried finding a better approach. Hot fear consumed his capacity for reasoning and he froze.

"I don't wanna shoot you, Gus," Homer lied from somewhere and Gus bolted. Maybe he didn't want to shoot Gus because a shot would announce their whereabouts. "We can work this out," he thought that he'd heard Homer say, but couldn't be sure because that's what bad guys always said.

The long way around the backside of egg rock, his heavy legs were slowing fast. Lungs burned for air.

He lunged from the low end of a rock wall. The drop was somewhere around four feet but felt like a long weightless freefall worthy of someone like Rambo. Time slowed as Gus lifted his arms. The moon backlighting his landing. Momentarily astonished at his triumphant and daring acrobatics, Gus paused and looked up. The huge guy was on him before he could move.

They went down heavy and hard. Gus on his back. Homer on top. A scream stuck in Gus's throat and the gun stuck in his grip.

With his finger wedged on the trigger, he thumbed the safety, but had no idea if he'd freed it. Homer sat up. Straddled Gus like a fat kid on a pony. Suddenly, a right hook nailed Gus in the jaw. A crunch followed by a searing pain that ran from his cheek, into his eyeball, and up to his brain. Maybe that was what knocked his superpowers free.

Gus struggled and wiggled and writhed like his life depended on it. No way he'd die without a fight and rolled sideway just enough to get his opposite hand on the gun.

The rabid beast bent over and growled as he wrapped his strong fingers around Gus's throat and squeezed. This was a terrible way for a hero to die. With both hands, Gus pulled the gun under Homer. Tilted it up and shoved it as hard as he could into the dense gut and pulled the trigger.

The muzzled blast split open the night and shook them apart. Gus's ears seemed to explode inside, although Homer's blubber had worked like a silencer and the gunfire was little more than a bang. Homer released his grip from around Gus's throat.

Heat engulfed Gus and the fat man came down hard. Pinned him like a bad wreck. His hand and gun and finger on the trigger stuck in place under the dead weight. Gus coughed and gulped one ragged breath after another. Homer howled, then bellowed like a wounded animal right next to Gus's ear.

The sound was excruciatingly painful. Why wasn't he dead already?

Gut shot. The worst way to die, Gus remembered. Maybe he should shoot him again. Finish him off. Put him out of his misery like he would any suffering creature. Any suffering decent creature, of which this guy was not. He'd tried to kill Gus. And Walter. Plus, he'd polluted the creek, poached a calf, and stolen Gloria. He was definitely no good.

Being gut shot was the best way for a bad guy to die. It took every bit of strength and much too much time for Gus to work his way out from under the heap of dying fat. But Gus couldn't give up. Couldn't die from being smushed by a bad guy. Imagine being found dead under Homer. What would Gloria think?

"No way." Being choked or shot would have been much better. He tried rolling Homer off. With all his might he shoved and pushed and the big lug didn't budge. Gus took a break and caught his breath.

"Help," Homer muttered.

"Get off," Gus answered. And the mass moved. Homer tilted in a feeble attempt to roll over. Although he came back down, Gus had freed his shoulders and wormed his way out. Fresh blood smeared the front of his favorite jacket. Panting, he got to his hands and knees.

Homer jerked and twisted up onto his side, reminding Gus of a kid on the school bus back in the fifth grade.

The boy had been sitting next to him, and then he wasn't. He was in the aisle—his arms punching and legs kicking at nothing. It scared Gus. Every time he closed his eyes, he'd see the kid on the floor like the world's worst dancer. Gus's mom and dad—his real mom and dad— explained that the kid had suffered a seizure. They decided the reason Gus had been so upset was because he had felt helpless and Gus agreed. After taking a CPR and first aid class, Gus hadn't thought of that kid, until now.

Homer clutched his gut and his face grimaced red as blood blossomed across his front. The sight of it tormented Gus, just like the kid on the bus. More and more blood seeped from Homer's mouth, then spewed like vomit as he coughed. Gus gagged and almost vomited himself. Killing bad guys wasn't at all easy or fun—even if they deserved it. The dying man's big brown eyes burrowed into Gus. He was in pain and moaned and Gus couldn't take it one more second. He wished the guy would just hurry up and die. The best thing to do would be to put a bullet between his eyes, but instead Gus crawled away with the gun in his hand and tears in his eyes.

"I'm sorry," Gus cried. He crawled back the way he'd come. Back around the tabletop granite. Back to the dead log. He sat up. Rested his back against it. Then brought his knees to his chest and wrapped his arms around them. His jaw felt like it had grown a softball inside it. Some superhero he was, he thought. Killing bad guys wasn't just hard work, it was terrible, awful work. The worst thing he'd ever done. Soon his sobs drowned out Homer's pitiful moans.

The time had come to pull himself together and save Miss Mo.

"I'm sorry." He was talking to God, not Homer. It came down to good versus evil, and good had finally won. It was God's will. Gus laced his fingers in prayer. He knew God would forgive him if he asked. If he'd repent.

"Dear Lord, forgive me." He prayed.

Once Homer quit moaning, Gus began to feel a little bit better. After replaying what he'd done over and over again in his mind he felt kind of good. Nothing worth doing is ever easy, his dad always said, and Gus had believed it then and he believed it now. His head nodded involuntarily.

"I am…a hero," he told himself and stood. Taking extra deep breaths, he forced himself away from the log and back to Homer. Back to the scene of the crime. Gus had never killed anyone, let alone seen a dead person, except for his dad. At the funeral, he looked like he did napping on the couch watching football. He looked happy and probably was since he got to go to heaven.

Gus looked around. Back and forth. Blinking, he forced his focus with wide eyes. His gun ready in his right hand, awkwardly he used his left to pull the headlamp from his coat pocket. He pressed it on and shined it down, illuminating blood and any doubt that he was in the wrong location. Homer was gone.

PART III
Chapter Twenty

Light seized me like a magnetic pull. There she stood, emanating a brilliant aura as she waved. Smiling like always.

"Maureen." Kate pressed her hand over her heart and teared up. "I found you. Finally."

She'd come for me, and every fiber of my being wanted to run to her. The urge to hug and kiss her demanded I hurry, but it was like trying to run in a dream. Impossible. Nothing worked right. I stumbled downstream toward her. Toward the light.

"Kate," I screamed, but it was all in vain.

"Kate," I muttered as my lips stiffened.

"Wait. Please." I love you. I had to tell her just once before death silenced me forever. Smart, strong, brave, and loving Kate deserved to know how much she'd meant to me. I'd never wanted anything more.

"Maureen." Kate doesn't call me Maureen.

The toothy smile was big. Too big. Nothing at all like Kate's.

"Holy smokes, you must be Maureen. Boy oh boy, am I glad to see you." He reached for me. I flinched and stumbled backwards.

"It's okay. I'm here to help you." A heavy jacket hung over his thin torso. Why was he so happy? Abnormally happy.

"We've been looking all over for you." He stepped toward me. "Please let me help you." He held out his upturned hands like you might in an attempt to capture a rabid dog. "I found your clothes."

I wanted his help. Wanted to say yes, please, help me. Save me. But the words were lost somewhere between my brain and my uncooperative lips.

He removed his backpack, unzipped it, and dug inside as if he were desperate to locate something significant. He plucked out my underwear. "Probably should put these on first. They're damp, but it'll be okay." Then he produced my pants.

He knelt at my feet and dressed me. I succumbed fully to helplessness when he pulled my underwear up, then my pants. "There you go. How's that?" He looked like he expected an answer. "Okay, then."

Before I knew it had happened, my bra, tank top, and hoodie were on. Time was playing out in fragmented pieces. Jumping ahead in jarring motion like broken and patched film documenting my fairytale ending.

The man removed his heavy green coat and I noticed a US Forest Service patch on the chest before he wrapped it around me. Tucked my arms inside the warm sleeves then zipped it up as far as it would go. When he pulled the collar up around my neck, his red hair and freckled face became familiar. I'd met him somewhere at some point, but couldn't pull up the entire memory. I wanted to thank him. At the very least, offer an appreciative smile, but couldn't.

A violent storm roused me from neither here nor there as he shook open a silver foil emergency blanket. Like wrapping a beach towel around a shivering toddler, he swung the thing up in the air and it floated down around me.

"You poor thing. It's going to be all right," he promised and proceeded to tighten then tie the corners of the blanket around my neck like a cape. "We'll figure something out." Like a miniature knight in dull green armor, he carried me to his quad and set me ever so gently on the seat. From a toolbox attached to the front of the quad, he brought out a first aid kit and cleaned my head wound with something.

"There you go. That's better." Suddenly my head was wrapped.

"Delores? Come in. I've *found* the missing hiker." It sounded accusatory, as if it were my fault. Like I'd wandered off the trail and gotten myself lost. Sure, I was lost now, but I hadn't caused the man to shoot Walter. Nor was it my fault people were cultivating marijuana illegally in the forest. I should be able to go fishing anytime I wanted and not have to worry about being killed. I would tell him this, all of it, but not now. Later. With Kate by my side. I closed my eyes.

"Delores! Come in. I need immediate instruction." No one answered. Delores had likely gone home for the night. It seemed like days had passed without sunlight.

"Deelooooresss?" the fellow sang. "I know you can hear me." He waited, staring at the radio as if willing it to respond. "Fine. Be that way." He hooked the radio back onto his belt and rubbed his chin. My feet dangled to one side, and with an exasperated effort, he scooted me forward on the seat. Straddled in behind me on the quad, and started the engine. As he thumbed the throttle, I leaned back, resting against his chest. My eyes refused to stay open and I lost track of reality.

The back-and-forth motion and soft rumble of the motor cast me between this world and the next. Both were warm and I had no regard as to which way I went. It was no longer up to me. I was too empty to care until I realized the quad had stopped. Something familiar awoke with the essence of skunk. I opened my eye. My rescuer lifted me off the quad and set me on the ground against a wall of burlap weed bundles. He took back the emergency blanket and balled it up.

No. No! No! No. I wanted to scream but could only moan. My savior unzipped and removed the warm coat he'd so gallantly placed upon me. It was simply too obvious. Completely predictable. They'd never get away with producing this much marijuana in the forest without his assistance. I should have seen it. Should have known he was too good to be true. If I were reading the book or watching the film, I would have laughed out loud at the cliché. I tried but couldn't summon the strength.

"Someone killed Homer!" Lupe came at the Forest Service man fast. "He's dead!" The glare she threw at me cut like a dull knife.

Homer? Who's Homer? The man? The man I beat? I didn't kill him. I had seriously considered it, but I didn't kill anyone. Did I? Had cracking his head with mine killed him? I'd attacked him with the tree limb too. Maybe I did kill the man—Homer. If so, I am a murderer. Oh my God.

"What?" The man stepped back from her. "I don't understand. What happened?"

"Someone shot his goddamn guts out!" She crossed her arms. Shook her head.

"Who?" He sounded scared.

"Maybe—DEA, Hell's Angels. That Stockton crew ripped off Justin twice. Hmongs are trying to stake their claim? Cartoon Network? How the fuck should I know? You're supposed to be protecting us!"

With both hands, Lupe grabbed what little hair hung from under my gauze wrap and dragged me.

"I'm getting out of here!" Lupe jerked me hard and the wrap around my head loosened. She continued pulling me backwards as my scalp stretched, splitting the wound wide open. Warmth tingled my skull.

We stopped moving when my back was once again against the tree. My tree. "This whole thing is fucked!" She pointed her fingers like a pistol at the ranger. "*You* failed to protect us."

He held up his hands. "I'm sorry. I keep watch the best I can." He looked down. "Dang. I can't help that Homer was attempting to steal a few bundles and ran into someone. It was not a wise choice."

"He was not stealing! Fuck you. You don't know shit."

"What was he doing out in the middle of the day? You both know better."

"It was only two bundles. Like you don't stash a few."

"No. I don't." His eyes widened and his chin lowered. He looked angry. His breathing was loud and I suddenly remembered I'd met him last year while helping Kate move cattle.

"Let's move forward. You stay here. I think I can get all of this moved before dawn."

"Weed ain't worth dying for. And I ain't going down for

no one." She pulled my arms behind my back and secured me to the tree.

"I would know if law enforcement had arrived. No one is coming until daylight," he said.

"Get me the fuck out of here." She nodded and stood up to him. "Take me home, *now*."

"Just calm down. Please. Let's use our heads and think this through." He rubbed his chin, looked at me, then back at her. "You stay put and I'll take a load right now. You know the escape route if things get sideways. We cannot just leave all this weed." He walked away. "The faster we load it, the faster we can get out of here."

"I don't work for you," Lupe growled, but followed anyway.

They grabbed one bundle after another and stacked them behind the seat on a rear rack until there wasn't room for another. My savior turned sinner opened the toolbox attached to the front of the quad and brought out two straps. He and Lupe began strapping down the bundles.

"If you're not back in *one* hour. I'm gone." She stomped away from him and glared at me with obvious repugnance. The look resembled the look Rosemary had given me years ago. I knew I was done for.

"Save me." I gave the rotten ranger one last chance to redeem his soul before sacrificing me. He started the motor and drove away. I abandoned all hope. No one in the world besides the corrupt, knew I was here. No one but the damaged would witness or believe my dramatic ending.

The sound of the quad faded, and silence fell hard. Lupe disappeared into her tent, and I closed my eyes until I heard the sound of her feet stomping toward me. This is how I die. Please let it be swift and painless. I've suffered enough for one night.

She knelt in front of me. Like a cougar, she tore a long piece of duct tape with her sharp teeth, then suddenly paused. Startled, she spun her head sideways, then tweaked it. Straining to see something in the dark. She slapped the tape over my eyes as the blast of gunfire echoed through the camp.

"Fuck this!" It sounded like she stood and stepped back. "You keep your mouth shut about me. You never saw me—or else—I'll fucking find you and everyone you love. And it'll be bad. Very bad."

Another shot cracked the silence from somewhere in the distance, followed by the unmistakable crunching sound of her feet running away. Fast over pine needles and sticks that cracked and popped and faded.

Law enforcement was close and would eventually find me. I closed my eyes and floated toward the comforts of oblivion.

Chapter Twenty-One

Moonlight revealed Homer resting against the north side of the tabletop rock. Homer might have already been dead, but Gus couldn't be sure and fired without hesitation. His aim was high and the bullet tore through Homer's neck, sending his head backwards. Gus surged closer and fired again. The bullet pierced his chest and Homer fell onto his side without reacting.

Gus shined his light at the mess. There wasn't much blood and he was thankful for that, but as he neared the body, an unmistakable stench of poop clobbered him like an outhouse on a hot day. Gus pulled his coat up over his nose and knew for sure that Homer was dead. Not only had he pooped his pants—his mouth hung open in a weird slant. Under his moustache, his gapped teeth reminded Gus of the rotting and peeling picket fence that bordered the flower garden back home at the buffalo ranch. What did Gloria see in this guy? If she figured out what Gus had done to her stupid, ugly boyfriend, she would definitely go berserk.

It was done. Nothing Gus could do about it now. He put

his headlamp in one coat pocket and his gun in the other. Leaving a dead body just lying around in the forest was stupid. If Homer wasn't found, people, including Gloria, might think he just wanted a better life and disappeared on his own.

Hiding him would be difficult. Dragging him would be impossible. First, he needed to locate the perfect hiding place. Somewhere close. Gus looked around. Wished he could get Homer to the big crevice behind the egg-shaped rock. No one would ever find him in there. But this guy was too big and the crevice too far.

"Think," Gus tapped the top of his head, "think." He bounced on his toes. "Come on." His jaw tightened and didn't hurt half as bad as before. He paced east until he reached the precipice. The edge of the cliff. If he couldn't drag him, he might be able to roll him. It looked to be less than fifty yards. He had to try.

Gus rushed back to the corpse. He needed to straighten him out and aim him in the right direction. Gus stood with his back to Homer's boots, then bent and grabbed them. With a tight grip on his feet, he lifted and tucked a foot under each armpit. Next, he crossed his arms. With his arm held tight against the man's ankles, Gus used his weight to maneuver the body.

Once he was in position, Gus moved around the back of Homer. When he dropped to his hands and knees, Gus caught a whiff of the excrement the bowels had released upon death. From then on, Gus breathed through his mouth and tried not to think about the smell. With all his might, he pushed the man from his lower back. To his surprise, the carcass rolled. Gus kept shoving. Pushing. Harder and faster until momentum kicked in and they reached the edge.

"Sorry." Gus reared up to his knees and rolled Homer off the edge, but didn't watch. The sound was bad enough, like a rock when it breaks free in the middle of a quiet night and crashes down. It was over in no time and suddenly he wanted to cry. Again. He looked up at the starless sky and took a breath. The man in the moon smiled at him. Gus smiled back.

He had to stay focused on his mission and tried hard to erase the picture of dead Homer from his mind, but it was impossible. The more he thought about not thinking about it, the more he thought about it. The heavy realization sparked the possibility that things like this were just what drove people insane. He hurried back to Benny. Next time his mind wandered onto the blast or the acrid smell of burnt gunpowder, or the sight of blood gurgling out of Homer's mouth, Gus replaced the thought.

It was during one of the worst Gloria sessions that Miss Mo taught Gus a cool little trick. She called it changing the channel. If you don't like what you're seeing, tune into something else. Most of the time, Gus had trouble finding the remote, but not this time. He tuned into an elaborate fantasy. He closed his eyes and saw himself march into the Wells Fargo bank with a wheelbarrow full of cash and buy back the ranch. The scene played over and over in his mind with the perfect Hollywood ending.

Benny brayed in the distance and Gus recoiled, then bolted the best he could. Fast from the cliff and back across the granite mountaintop to a section of skinny pines. There he laid flat. Scoured the area for movement. Listening for a clue as to what had caused Benny's alarm. Nothing. Not a sound except for his own breathing heartbeat.

Slowly, he stood. Benny brayed again as Gus pulled the gun from his pocket, remembered to release the safety, and raced ahead. As he neared the downed log where he'd left Benny, he slowed. Swept the gun back and forth. Ready for whatever was out there.

"Gus?"

Gus spun. The gun in his hand. His arm straight and rigid.

He knew the voice.

"What the hell are you doing here?" She sounded mad and her eyes bulged like they might explode at any minute.

"Gloria." Gus forced a smile. "I mean...Lupe." Gus shook his head. Did she know what he'd done to her Homer?

"You can drop the alias. What's the point?" Gloria stepped toward him. Gus lowered his gun. "So what the fuck you up to?" she asked.

"I...I...I'm making sure...you...don't get busted." He doubted she believed his lie.

"Why didn't you use the radio and call 'Delores'?" She made finger quotes because there was no "Delores." Delores was code for something's wrong and everyone better listen. Miss Mo's black and orange hat hung on Gloria's finger.

Gloria knew when anyone lied. Like she had a lie detector hidden inside of her. He cleared his throat. "I forgot...to turn it...off. The batteries died...and...the new ones...are at my mom's. Sorry." He pasted a puzzled look on his face. "Are you...okay?"

"I heard gunshots. Someone killed Homer."

"Oh no!" Gus gasped and covered his mouth. "I heard the...shots...too."

"You see anyone?"

"Two...guys...I think...they were...deputies." Gus shook his head and tried to look scared. He squinted and let his mouth fall. "I had to...warn you."

"Fuck." Gloria bent over onto her knees. "Fuck. I knew it. They killed Homer." She sounded more scared than sad. "This is a nightmare, Gus. If I go back to prison, Mandy will take me out."

"I know." Gus rubbed her back. "You...should go. Get...out of here...while you...can."

Gloria straightened and sighed.

"Where is...Miss Mo?" Gus asked.

"In camp. She's fine. We should have left her where she fell. Let the bitch die. Now, because of her, we're fucked."

"Gloria." Gus looked into her eyes. He loved those big brown doe eyes and seriously considered telling her about the old mine. He could give her directions and the key to the gate. She could wait there for him. She'd be safe. He stroked her long hair and she stepped back.

"Don't fucking touch me." Her nostrils flared like the mad cow that had attacked Gus.

"I love you...but you...are a bad...person."

"Fuck you. So are you." She snarled. Her thick eyebrows came together. The mad cow was about to attack.

"If...I ever...see you...again...I will...kill you." Gus snatched Miss Mo's hat from Gloria's hand. Then he turned and walked away from the love of his life.

"What the fuck's that supposed to mean?"

Gus did not look back.

"You're gonna kill me? Seriously?" She laughed. "You?"

Tears filled his eyes. Walking away from her had just become the hardest thing he'd ever done. More than a million dollars, in that moment, he wanted so badly to turn around. Hug her soft skin and kiss her yummy lips.

"Did you check with your Magic 8 Ball? That what it told you to do? Huh? Ya fucking idiot!"

Her words cut him beyond repair. He wasn't an idiot,

only a child of incest, which made him feel even worse. An idiot wouldn't understand or care that he was an idiot—therefore, actually being an idiot would be far less depressing.

"And don't worry dickhead, you won't *never* see me again! I'm outta here."

Emotion boiled into a mix of hurt and anger. He fingered the gun and fought back tears as a rock seemed lodged in his throat. He swallowed and swallowed down the pain. No way he could ever hurt Gloria. He loved her and slipped the gun back into his fanny pack.

Being nuzzled by his furry friend comforted Gus. He kissed and hugged Benny instead of Gloria.

"Let's go, buddy." He untied Benny and led him around the downed log. "Miss Mo…is waiting…for us."

There was no way to avoid the tabletop rock, but Gus found the farthest and lowest approach for himself and Benny. They stepped in rhythm. The soothing clip-clop of hooves on rock was familiar. Gus yawned.

For once, he recognized that he'd made a good decision and was glad he hadn't put shoes on Benny's feet. Steel shoes were loud and made slipping much easier while climbing smooth granite. Gus jumped off the two-foot tall table rock and let the lead rope fall. Benny dropped his head and studied the distance below before deciding whether or not to jump. The donkey landed effortlessly and Gus picked up his rope. There was no path. Together they trudged through a jungle of manzanita, madrone, and mountain misery. Sorrow weighing him down.

Gus smelled the campfire and knew he was near. He tugged Benny along.

The marijuana nugget he'd eaten earlier had kicked in. His jaw didn't hurt all that bad anymore, but now his arms were numb and his heart jackhammered in his chest. He tied Benny to a solid branch, then slipped the gun out of his fanny pack. After a few shallow breaths, he approached the weed camp. "You got this," he told himself. "Use…the pain…for good. For Miss Mo."

Gus moved through the timber without making a sound and disrupting the silence. Maybe the sheriff's department or DEA had arrived and might shoot him. Maybe that would serve him right for lying to Gloria.

Stepping softly, slowly, heel first, avoiding sticks that would crack. All while using the trees and darkness for cover. Zigzagging from a cedar to pine. From pine to a spruce. He took one last deep breath—and held it.

It was as if someone had shoved fishing weights down his gullet and he couldn't budge. Like his feet or legs had suddenly become too heavy to move. He thought of Miss Mo. Would she think he was brave?

It was now or never. He spit. "You got this."

He thundered in.

The lady sitting under the narrow cedar shocked, then scared the heck out of him. She didn't even look at all like Miss Mo. Her face was way too fat and her color was all wrong. She was filthy from her head to her toes and looked more like some sort of zombie than a living, breathing human. Gray duct tape covered her eyes. Maybe Gus had screwed up again. Had they captured another woman wandering through the woods?

The zombie lady lifted her head. Silver strands just like Miss Mo's shone under her matted hair.

"Miss Mo!" Gus didn't mean to scream, it just came out the moment he recognized her. His heart dropped, then felt like someone had grabbed it and was wringing it out.

Miss Mo moaned. "Help."

"Miss Mo."

He went to her and knelt.

"It's me, Gus." Dirty dried blood stained the side of her neck and her peach hoodie. Gus grabbed his headlamp and shined it onto the side of Miss Mo's head. The gash along her temple probably needed stitches, but the blood had caked and scabbed and was no longer bleeding.

"You'll be...okay." Gus wanted to hug her, but instead pulled out his pocketknife and freed her arms. She started to fall onto her side and Gus caught her. He hugged her. "I got you." He peeled back a corner of the duct tape covering her eyes and pinched it tight. "Hold on." He ripped the tape off just like his mom ripped off Band-Aides.

"Hi." Gus said.

Miss Mo cracked one eye open. The white part was blood red like it was bleeding. It looked terrible—painful—and made Gus grimace. He forced a grin close to her face. A bruise colored her cheekbone just under her left eye. "You're...okay. It's Gus."

Miss Mo stared at him like she was someplace else.

"Where are...your shoes and socks?"

Miss Mo only winced when Gus held her up. "They hid...them so...you...couldn't run...away." That's when he smelled it and realized Miss Mo had wet her pants.

"It's okay." Miss Mo collapsed and Gus caught her before she hit the ground. "I got you." She was heavy for such a skinny lady and he laid her on her side.

"I'll be...right back." Gus ripped off his coat and covered Miss Mo's shoulders. A chill engulfed him, but he'd never felt more like a hero as he hurried to the forest green tent. Homer and Gloria's tent.

Inside, he found a puffy red sleeping bag and snatched it up. "Perfect." He trotted back to Miss Mo with the bag and laid it out at her feet. First, he unzipped it, then gently stuffed her feet into the bag. They were like ice. He worked the silky bag up her legs all the way to her hips. It must have felt nice to her, because she wiggled herself down into the bag as Gus worked it up. His coat was on the ground and he wanted to put it back on, but a good guy would not do that. He picked up his coat, gave it a good shake, and zipped it around Miss Mo.

Once the sleeping bag was up and around her shoulders, Gus zipped it as far as it would go. "Like a…caterpillar. When you emerge…you will…be a butterfly." Miss Mo closed her eyes. Gus touched her head. "Okay. You're… okay."

The fire was nearly out and allowed Gus to catch a whiff of the remaining cannabis. The stacked burlap bundles mesmerized him. That was a lot of money right there, Gus knew. More than enough to buy back his buffalo ranch and get his mom out of that terrible trailer. He marched to the stump where the religious candle flame flickered and blew it out.

Chapter Twenty-Two

Hauling all that weed back to camp and saving Miss Mo would be impossible. Gus had to choose one or the other, but not both. There was no way he could move all those bundles by himself before morning even if he didn't have to save Miss Mo. He had all but given up on taking the weed when the idea of compromise struck.

"Miss Mo?"

She did not respond. Maybe she was dead. "Miss Mo?" Gus gently shook her shoulder until she opened her one good eye and looked at him. "You okay?" he asked, but Miss Mo still didn't respond. "Are you okay to rest... here while I do...something?" She closed her one good eye and nodded. "Okay...I'll be fast."

Gus left Miss Mo asleep in the sleeping bag next to the fire. She seemed comfortable and Gus would either complete his mission fast or he'd forget about it and get on with saving Miss Mo. Ten or fifteen extra minutes would probably not make any difference to Miss Mo, but could make all the difference in the world to Gus and his mom.

Inside Gloria and Homer's tent, Gus flipped on his headlamp and began tossing items outside as fast as he could. A backpack went first, then a sleeping bag, followed by a cot and three pillows. With the radio in his hand, he went outside and hurled it to the ground. He stomped on it too many times to count until it broke beyond repair. The portable propane heater he carried out and set to the side because it seemed wasteful to throw and break such a valuable item.

Lastly, he gathered up the pile of their dirty clothes and tossed them into the fire. He watched them smolder until he remembered he had to hurry. Miss Mo was waiting. He checked to make sure she was still okay. She looked about as peaceful as anyone sleeping could look, so he went back to the tent.

Working quickly, Gus unhooked the rainfly cover and slid it onto the ground. Next, he pulled the stakes and tent poles free. The tent collapsed and fell to earth like a deflating hot air balloon. Gus dragged the tent to the stack of remaining weed and began loading bundles through the door flap as if he were bagging groceries.

When the tent was heavy, but not too heavy, Gus zipped the door shut. He'd lost count of the bundles, but guessed he'd loaded at least thirty, maybe even forty. With each bundle weighing around five pounds and outdoor-grown weed being sold at an average of one-thousand dollars per pound, give or take, that made each bundle worth five thousand dollars. Calculating a minimum of thirty bundles, Gus's haul was worth at the very least—

"One hundred...fifty thousand...dollars," Gus said as he gathered the rainfly off the ground. With that much money, there was a good chance he would have the ranch back by spring. He towed the tail of the fly and the tent over his shoulder like a hillbilly Santa. Dragging his treasure away from the grow camp as fast as he could.

Down an embankment, the tent snagged a tree and twice Gus had to manipulate the giant weed-filled sack between boulders. Frustration grew as he struggled to hurry. The plan was to get the goods to the deep crevice below the egg-shaped rock. It would make a good dry hiding place and Gus could return later, soon as it was safe. But at this rate of speed, he wouldn't get there anytime soon and Miss Mo needed off this mountain right now.

He stopped, wiped the sweat from his brow, and scrutinized the area. There had to be a decent hiding place close by. Nothing but trees, mountain misery, and dead timber left few options. Sometimes hiding in plain sight was the best tactic, and considering the situation, Gus had no choice.

He moved fast, flattening out the tent and spreading the bundles out evenly. Once he had them situated, he rolled the entire thing like a big green nylon tortilla. Over and over, creating a long weed burrito, wedged against an ample downed cedar.

Gus covered the giant weed burrito with the green rain-fly, tucking it in and under on all sides to keep the bundles dry when it rained or snowed. Next, he tossed every branch and variety of moveable timber on top to camouflage the whole thing. When he stepped back and examined his work, he nodded. Moving and hiding the weed had only taken an extra twenty minutes. Longer than he'd hoped, but Miss Mo would be okay. Gloria had said she was fine even though she didn't really look fine.

Walking away, he turned around twice and looked back at his hidden treasure to see if it seemed out of place. The last time he looked back, he made up his mind that odds were better than good his weed would not be found. Not because it was a good hiding place or that the green tent blended into the background so well, it was mostly because no one would look.

Chapter Twenty-Three

The first blue light of morning had conquered the dark when Kate awoke in Gus's bedroll, coughing. For a moment, she didn't know where she was or that Mo was missing. She looked up at the smoke hole in the top of the teepee and shivered as it all flooded back and drowned her. Yesterday morning, Mo's text had put a smile on her sleepy face—*Last chance to fish!!!*

Now only grief. Odds were better than good that Mo was dead. Yesterday seemed like years ago, and a hollow ache clawed at her stomach as she curled onto her side.

"Come here, Walter." The mutt looked up at her with his liquid brown eyes. She would take him home and try to love him as much as Mo did.

"Come on." Kate held back the blanket, and Walter joined her. She removed a pine needle stuck to the sap on his ear and covered him. Wrapped an arm around the dog and snuggled him from behind. He would mourn Mo too. Kate would have cried if she had the energy and closed her eyes. Mo's face filled the darkness. Her soft brown eyes always smiled more than her mouth. Her gentle, almost childlike laugh that was the flip side of Kate's. With time, memories would fade despite any refusal to let them.

Mulling over the past never helped, but that didn't stop Kate. If only she'd gone fishing with Mo, they'd both be home drinking coffee, talking on the phone—if only.

"Kate..." The panic in Mo's voice the last time they spoke played in her mind with a searing pain. *"Kate, help..."* Her heart throbbed and she fumbled out of the bedroll. The fire had died and her hot heaving cough clouded the dull light. She searched and found the bottle of water, but it was empty.

"Kate." She couldn't stop the screaming in her head as she stood rubbing her wet eyes. Walter lifted his head and pricked his good ear.

"Kate." She felt for the pistol in her pocket. It was there. Soon the sun would rise and reveal the reality of what was to come. In less than a minute, Kate was outside the teepee with the empty bottle. The last of the moon shined down on Forest Creek. Water flowed louder—faster and murky from last night's rain, but she crouched and drowned the plastic bottle anyhow. As it filled, the scent of wet pine overwhelmed and nauseated her. She finally admitted, if only to herself, that she was ill. A reaction to the vaccine she determined, and gulped down the icy creek water from the bottle. It numbed her cough and she refilled it.

"Kate." The voice would not cease. An incurable madness had crept in and with Mo gone there was little hope. Cold bit as she crouched—doubtful she'd ever feel warm again. She'd had her chance and would suffer the consequences.

"Kate." The voice gained strength as Kate stood. Took another swig from the bottle.

"Kate." She searched the tall timber, past the creek, through the gray dawn.

Wind blew just enough to add character to the forest. "Kate." It was only the wind mixed with her own constant craving.

"Kate." She caught movement across the creek and adjusted her focus. Chills prickled as she wiped her wet palms on her thighs and tilted her head sideways as if it would improve her vision.

A malformed shadow emerged from the trees, clopping. She heard the clopping of hooves. She was sure of it. Closer and closer to the creek. Kate adjusted her eyes. Held her breath as she strained to see it. To listen. She stepped toward the creek, then remembered the bear and thought better of it. She waited. And watched.

The world stood still as Joseph emerged, leading the donkey from the forest. The Virgin Mary robed in a red sleeping bag rode rigid as they crossed the creek.

"Holy fuck." There was no deciphering reality as a star twinkled above and Gus stumbled into the creek. Kate's hands covered a gasp. Chills prickled the back of her neck.

"Grammy Kate!" he yelled midstream.

Kate couldn't move. Couldn't trust her own eyes or her sanity. Her heart had found its way to her throat and choked her. Tears stung her nose and eyes as the possibility that the vision was real slowly sunk in.

"Kate." Mo looked ghostly but spoke.

"Mo?" Kate dropped her water bottle. "Mo." She rushed into the creek. "Mo!"

Kate touched Benny's neck and the red sleeping bag. Felt Mo's leg beneath it. Solid. The apparition was real.

They stepped out of the creek.

"Are you hurt?" Kate asked.

"She will...be okay." Gus's rubber boots splashed out of the creek.

From atop Benny, Mo reached out for Kate.

"Oh my God! Oh my God! Mo." Kate wrapped her arms around Mo's waist and helped her down. One side of Mo's face was caked with dried blood and her skull wrapped in bloody gauze. She had an eye that resembled an overripe plum and was swelled shut. Dirt and dried blood drew a line from her nose and ringed the open mouth she breathed through. With a split upper lip and a broken front tooth, Kate cradled Mo's face.

"*I* love you." Kate's wide eyes became wild. She never broke eye contact. "You understand me?" Kate held Mo's face. "I *love* you." Kate kissed her gently, then pressed her forehead against Mo's and wept.

Mo's blank stare and blood crusted lips parted. "Ow."

"I'm sorry. So, so, sorry." Kate held Mo's hand.

Smiling seemed to be an effort, and Mo closed her eyes. She lifted her arms and wrapped the sleeping bag around them both. For a long while the women held each other tight as they could and shared a wordless understanding that from here on out nothing would ever be the same.

Walter whined and sneezed and jumped on Mo.

"Walter," Mo managed. She knelt and rubbed his head. "Oh, my honey." Walter spun circles and cried and bounced with an uncontainable love.

"I think the bullet split his ear, but Gus fixed him up," Kate said, as Mo sat on the ground and cried. She laughed and embraced Walter as he licked her bad eye. With a big, bright smile, Mo looked up at Gus and Kate. "This is the best day of my life."

"Mine too." Kate hugged Gus and kissed the top of his head. "Mine too." She sat down beside Mo and wrapped her arm around her. Mo turned to Kate and leaned in for a proper kiss. Kate didn't hesitate. It was like tasting freedom. Love, in its purest form made from a conscious choice. The choice she would have made long before the world told her who she should be. A mutual admiration for being given a second chance.

"What the hell happened out there?"

Mo teared up and Kate wished she hadn't asked. Why put her through it now? Now she needed a hospital, not the third degree, for Christ's sake. "Never mind. I—you need pain killers. I don't have anything. Gus, what do you have in the way of pain meds?"

"I have...something." Gus reached into his fanny pack and scooped out a handful of green nuggets. "You can...eat them. They will...help."

"What is it?" Kate asked.

"Weed." He pinched three nuggets into his opposite hand.

"You told me you don't smoke that shit."

"I don't." Gus handed Mo the nuggets and she put them in her mouth and chewed.

Kate didn't like the idea of getting high, but this wasn't the time or place for debate. She hoped it helped ease Mo's pain.

"I'll get you some water." Kate stood, rushed to the shore, and retrieved the bottle she'd dropped. She trotted back, handed it to Mo, and watched her down the entire bottle.

"Want more?" Kate asked, and Mo nodded. "Oh shit. Shit. Hope I'm not contagious. I've been coughing, but I think it's just a reaction to the shot. Like Roper had, but the last thing you need is to get fucking Covid."

"I'll live," Mo smiled, "or die happy."

"This is why I love you."

"I'll...get water. I have...good water." Gus took the bottle inside his teepee.

"Kate?"

Kate leaned in. "What?"

"Would you go on a date with me?" Mo looked up at Kate expressionless.

Kate grinned, sat down next to Mo, and held her close. Mo laid her head on Kate's lap. "Soon as you get better, we're not only going on a date, we're going camping, fishing, hiking, whatever the hell you want. I promise." She meant it.

Mo smiled and closed her good eye as Kate gently wiped away dirt and debris from her cheek.

Gus returned with a bottle of clean water and set it next to Mo.

"Gus, can you call Danny K. on the radio and tell him to get us out of here?" Kate asked.

Gus shook his head, like a kid refusing to eat his lima beans. "Not...a good...idea."

"Why not?"

"He is...a bad guy."

"What?"

"He came to the camp," Mo said, taking forever to get the words out between breaths, "to transport the cannabis. I assume he also kept watch for them. I remembered him from when you and I gathered cattle last year."

"You've got to be shitting me." Kate looked up at Gus.

"Nope." Gus scratched his head. "He is...very bad."

"That no-good son-of-a-bitch. Now I know why he was in no hurry to help. Fucking asshole. I'll kill him." Kate stood, looked directly at Gus, and crossed her arms. "We in danger?"

Gus raised his brow and looked at the sky as if it held the answer. "I will check...my Magic 8 Ball." He hurried back to the teepee and went inside.

"We should go. Can you ride or walk?"

"How far?" Mo looked doubtful.

"I think about three miles. Maybe closer to four."

Mo didn't answer. She looked at her bare feet. "I can probably ride."

"I know!" Kate clapped her hands. "That thing. What's it called? That deal the Natives hooked to their horses to carry stuff. Like a stretcher." Kate bounced around, pinching the space between her eyebrows. "Ummm."

"A travois?" Mo asked.

Gus came back with the 8 Ball in his hand. "It is... decidedly so."

"What?"

"We...are in...danger."

"You know what a travois is?" Kate asked Gus.

"Of course..." Gus furrowed his face.

"Can we make one and hook it to Benny?"

Gus smiled and tossed his Magic 8 Ball to Grammy Kate. "Heroes...can...do anything."

Chapter Twenty-Four

Watching Gus and Kate fuss over how best to situate me in the sleeping bag and then into the hammock left little question of how much they cared. Walter slept alongside me. Kate ran to the teepee, then returned with a heavy wool blanket and covered me and Walter. The security and warmth were bittersweet. I hated seeing them go to all the trouble, but being cared for felt better than a fish on a fly rod. I considered their action from the previous night. Kate told me how she'd searched and worried herself sick over me, but more importantly, what she failed to mention was how she placed her life at risk to find me, knowing full well there was a man with a gun.

Kate didn't wait for someone else to get around to looking for me. She did it herself. She and Gus. Gus, my hero and savior, gave his all to rescue me. I assumed based on their actions from last night that they truly loved me. Until that moment, I'd never fully realized how terribly I lacked that one human connection that even animals possess. I was no longer cold.

"Hungry? Want a granola bar?" Kate offered. "It's a soft chewy one."

I nodded and she fed me as Gus fed Benny grain from a burlap sack he'd hung from behind the donkey's ears to form a feedbag under his mouth.

"He will need...extra energy...to get back." Benny lowered his head to the ground and chomped grain as Gus disappeared into the trees behind me. Soon after, a chopping sound filled the fading darkness.

When I opened my eyes, the earth's rotation had smothered the moon and stars, allowing fragile grains of light to escape. With the light came budding potential. Exhilarated with love that came to me as unexpectedly as weed growers in the woods.

Walter jumped down when they lifted the sleeping bag with me in it and placed me on top of a canvas bedroll. They had crossed and strapped together two long pine poles —forming a V shaped ladder of sorts that didn't look sturdy enough to drag through the forest if it were empty. The travois sagged when they placed me on it and I felt a jerk. Next came a long pitch and a fast forward motion.

"Whoa." Gus held Benny and I came to an abrupt halt.

"Think he's gonna be okay?" Kate asked.

"He's never...pulled anything." Gus sounded concerned. Doubtful even.

"Maybe this isn't a good idea. If he takes off..." Kate stopped as Benny jumped and jigged and jerked me sideways. Kate held tight to the sleeping bag, but when Benny bucked and brayed, she dashed ahead of him. "Whoa, damn it!"

Gus was on the ground, and suddenly I was too. Walter ran for cover and watched the entire fiasco from a safe distance. Kate had Benny in a headlock as he bounced her off her feet—up and down toward the creek.

"Whoa—you counterfeit bastard!" Kate and Benny and the travois were nearing the creek. It was inappropriate, I know, but I could not help myself, and laughed as if I'd gone mad. Only Kate.

The release was beautiful as Kate got to her feet at the creek bank. In one swift motion, she snatched up Benny's lead, jerked him around so he was suddenly facing her. She flipped the travois off over his head. Freeing him from the monstrous contraption. The jackass ran across the creek and disappeared through the brush. Gus's eyes were wide and his mouth agape. He picked himself up off the ground and looked down at me while I cracked up. A smile broke his astonished face and he too found humor in the failure.

"What's so goddamn funny! That could have been a hell of a wreck. We just get you back and then kill ya. Hilarious, huh?" Kate stepped backwards, pulling the travois away from the creek. Gus ran to assist her.

It appeared the travois had survived as Kate got to me. "Maybe later I'll get a kick out of this, but not now. Now me and Gus are gonna have to haul your ass out of here." She grinned and I knew without a speck of doubt that she positively loved me.

"Hey," I said.

She stopped in her tracks and I reached for her hand. When she gave it, I squeezed. "I fucking love you, Kate."

"Yeah, yeah, yeah, I love you too, potty mouth." She grinned, kissed my hand, and got to work tucking me inside the canvas bedroll.

Gus helped Kate lift me back onto the travois.

"You okay?" Kate asked, and I nodded as Gus stepped behind the V and lifted the poles. Before I knew it, we were moving and Walter led the parade. The ride was smooth and the rocking motion like a cradle. Light revealed mountaintops that passed gradually as milestones.

"Let me know if it gets too heavy, Gus." Kate walked alongside me when the trail allowed—constantly glancing down at me.

"Gus, I'll take over whenever you need a break," she said.

"It's not…heavy." Gus didn't seem to put out much effort. "I got this…Grammy. Relax." He was strong and wise and I owed him my life.

"You're my hero, Gus. I love you," I said.

"I know. I…love you too." He picked up his pace.

Kate watched her brave grandson, who'd found the willpower to be a hero. I slept in peaceful slumber, knowing life would be good, no matter what, from here on out.

I shuddered as a sudden turbulence roused me from sweet slumber. My eye opened. A mountain lion watched from a boulder set back above the trail. Its bulging black eyes tracked us. She opened her massive jaw, flaunting her long, sharp fangs perfect for splitting flesh and bone. Then, like a witch, she wailed. Was it pain, grief, or anger? Had the others heard? Why hadn't they stopped? Silently, she leaped from one boulder to the next. The path narrowed as we climbed. Brush closing in. The lion gained on her prey and positioned herself behind the travois. I tried to scream, "She's stalking us!" but I couldn't speak. Couldn't move a muscle and realized what was happening. Another hypnopompic hallucination brought on by stress. The lion crouched, her tail flicking, ready to attack. All just a frightful figment of my imagination.

Reality came to life with the morning sun and lit my future with a brilliant light. It dawned on me that my book, *The Magic Outside Your Comfort Zone*, suddenly had more meaning than I could have imagined. I began piecing together my dramatic narrative. It would make a great story. My survival would likely inspire women around the world if I could get the events straight.

"We found her! She's alive!" Kate yelled as we approached the bridge at Forest Creek. Oddly, I thought of my bike as I watched Kate's eyes light up. She had suffered more than I, but I wondered if my bike was still hiding there behind the big boulder. Unable to see where I was going, only where I had been, as the tail end of the travois scraped and bounced across the wooden bridge. Footsteps came rushing. A few at first, then a mob.

"Is she okay?" The voice was familiar. "*Please* tell me she's okay." It was Roper. He'd grown up with Kate's daughter Em and was like family to her. I'd been treating him on and off for a few months and was surprised to see his smiling face when he looked down at me. "Oh my God," he put his hand on his heart, "am I glad to see you. We were so worried, hon," he said, tears filling his eyes. His lower lip quivered below his great teeth.

Jessica Williams's face popped up overhead, filling my limited vision. She looked different. "Maureen. My God, I'm so grateful you're okay." It was her hair. A classy shoulder-length cut, with messy auburn-colored curls. It complimented her strong jaw and freckles. My hair would never behave half as well.

She touched the top of the canvas bedroll and fought

back tears. "No more fishing alone. And we're going to have to discuss the guilt I feel for introducing you to fly fishing." She forced a laugh to cover up an unfounded responsibility for my ordeal.

"Make an appointment," I muttered.

Jessica laughed. "What a way to sell your book. With this ending, you mark my words—there'll be a bidding war."

"Huh, yeah," I said. It seemed possible. Probable even, the more I considered it as the glare of sunlight bit into my eye. I raised my hand and shaded my face.

The travois rumbled and jounced off the bridge then raked the rocky ground with the turbulence reminiscent of a wooden roller coaster. After a death-defying thrill ride, it came to an abrupt halt. Just like that, it was over. I could disembark and go on with my life. I sat up and looked forward.

A staging area had been set up just past the bridge. Groups gathered under two blue canopies. A dozen Calaveras County Sheriff vehicles were parked in a row. Trucks, SUVs, and cars, tucked into every available space. Strangers with dogs. Riders with horses. Backpackers. ATVs. Tables stocked with pink bakery boxes and trays of Saran-wrapped sandwiches. Long white ice chests lined the fronts of tables. Gus lowered the travois poles.

"August!" His mother rushed him. Her afro would not be contained under a chunky knit cap, and neither would her love for her son. She smiled, spread her arms wide as Gus ran to her. He closed his eyes as his real mom rocked him in her embrace. A match made in heaven.

The unmistakable whomp of an approaching helicopter did not distract my audience. Strangers held up phones, approached, and took my photo. Some kept their phones aimed at me, taking video I suspected.

A crowd of familiar smiling faces surrounded and over-whelmed me. Nearly every single patient I'd treated since coming to Calaveras was there. Samantha, the girl who'd been shot accidentally on purpose by her meth-dealing boyfriend. Kelly, Hawk, and Nicole, all battling addiction and probation. Marcus, who'd lit several forest fires, but came to me, open and honest about his arson. Isabelle Garcia, a former correc-tions officer contemplating divorce after forty years of marriage, had brought her husband whom she disliked.

There were at least two dozen more. I could not believe they'd all come to help me. Spending their precious time searching the woods was the last thing I'd have thought they'd do. An overdose of gratitude brought tears and a mix of emotion that eventually turned toward guilt. I had caused this massive operation. Me. All this because I needed to go fishing. I put everyone at risk. Before I could continue blaming myself, I dragged the absurd guilt file into the trash bin, heard the crumpling paper sound in my mind, and waved at a familiar face I had yet to place.

To say I was pleasantly surprised was the understate-ment of the century. These people were not only my patients and acquaintances, they were now my friends.

The travois lifted straight up like a magic carpet. I floated through the air with the help of what seemed to be everyone. Gus and his mother ate powdered sugar donuts with Walter. She waved as I passed.

Kate spoke to a group of sheriffs who seemed eager to hear whatever it was she had to say. Ed Manetti, the soon-to-be-ex-boyfriend, handed Kate a Gatorade, put his arm around her, and gave me a thumbs up. Who was watching the twins? They were fine, I assured myself, because Ed was a reliable, trustworthy, good man. I hated thinking he'd be hurt or heartbroken when Kate ended their relationship. I sincerely hoped we would remain friends.

There are so many things out of our control as we move through this world. Some are cursed with abusive parents or partners. Some are born with genetic defects. Some are the victims of random violence. Tragedies come in every size and shape. But with friends, those tragedies become manageable. I inhaled deep breaths of delicious, unburdened air. The world is a wonderful place if you work at it.

Chapter Twenty-Five

Gus felt the weight of heavy air press down and then a terrible pressure squeezed his chest as the pounding roar of the helicopter landed in a clearing just above the staging area. Gus's mom kissed and hugged and reassured him in front of everyone while he kept his hand over his ears and tried to focus on something positive. He thought about Gloria and wished he hadn't.

"Damn it," he yelled and people pretended not to notice.

"The helicopter is way up there. Look, Gus. It's pretty far away. And be glad it's here because it can take Miss Mo to the hospital really fast." Mom rubbed his back and it helped a little. The chopper quieted, and Gus removed his hands from his ears. The ache in his jaw kicked up, probably because he'd been clenching it for too long. From his fanny pack, he dug out the last bits of buds and swallowed them down.

He was happy to see his mom when she brought him a

sandwich. He needed to eat after all that hiking and saving people, but his jaw needed to quit hurting first.

"Let's go home, hon." Mom handed him a napkin.

"Not now." Gus went back to the food table and removed another sandwich from the Saran-wrapped tray. "I have to…get Benny…and break camp…before it…rains again. The teepee will be…too heavy…to pack out…when it's wet."

"It's supposed to rain tonight and last for a few days. After all you've been through, why don't you just leave it? We can get it another time." Her voice was sweeter than gummy worms and he considered it as he tore a piece of sandwich. The thought of a hot shower and Mom's cooking was tempting. He put the chunk of salami and bread in his mouth and chewed softly.

"Mom. I have…to take…care of…business." He grabbed two more sandwiches, wrapped them in napkins, and shoved them into his backpack.

"I love you." He kissed her cheek and everyone started clapping. Gus jumped, covered his ears again, and watched as Miss Mo rose up off the travois stretcher and stood on her bare feet. With Grammy Kate's help, she walked to a sheriff's SUV and they climbed into the back seat. Walter jumped in after them. When they pulled away up the hill to the helicopter, people cheered like they were at a rodeo watching the best bull ride ever. It was nice that everyone was so happy, but Gus wished they weren't so loud. He needed peace and quiet and promised his mom he'd see her tomorrow.

Benny was back from his rampage over the travois and braying when Gus arrived at camp.

"Hi, Ben." There was still plenty of daylight left after packing up the inside of the teepee. He napped in his hammock one last time. The nap turned into a deep sleep that lasted longer than Gus had planned. Exhaustion will do that to a person, but rested, he was ready to get back to business.

His Australian rain slicker would come in handy in case Mom was right and it stormed. He set it alongside his daypack with the Magic 8 Ball and extra matches. After reloading his gun magazine with the last six bullets, Gus threw the radio into the creek. Soon as he'd done it, he realized batteries were toxic and wasted a half an hour retrieving the darn thing. He'd dispose of it properly later on. It seemed like being a good guy took way more work than being a bad guy.

He boiled a pot of creek water to kill whatever crap might be polluting it and let it cool while dismantling the teepee. An hour later, storm clouds gathered and it smelled like rain. Gus was sweating but had rolled up the canvas teepee, tucked it behind some manzanita brush along with the hammock and his mining tools. He covered the pile with a camo-colored tarp, then stacked the teepee poles on top to keep it from blowing away.

Next, Gus saddled Benny with an old pack saddle and hung a canvas pannier off either side of the wooden forks. He filled the bags with his dirty clothes, muddy boots, trash, pots and pans, and his daypack, then strapped the bedroll and a shovel on top.

When his camp was spotless, Gus wrestled on his stiff slicker and headed west. Benny followed like a good dog. The animal knew when summer was over and it was time to leave. Benny wanted out of these cold wet mountains as much as Gus did, but first they had to backtrack two and a half miles.

Guilt took on a mind of its own as Gus neared the bottom of the cliff. He'd have left Homer there, but between God and law enforcement, Gus decided at the very least he should bury him. Moving the heavy body, now dead weight, in an attempt to conceal the crime was out of the question. Even with Benny's help, Gus couldn't come up with a scenario that worked. Burying him was the only right thing to do.

The exact location of the corpse was vague. Gus searched up and down the length of possibilities. Back and forth four times while Benny stayed put nibbling the last bit of dead grass. Gus looked up, wondering if the dude could have gotten caught in a tree or wedged behind a boulder. Maybe he hadn't rolled all the way down. But no, nothing as far as he could see.

"Well...if I can't...find him..." Neither could anyone else. Gus gave up and turned back the way he'd come.

"Let's go." He patted Benny on the neck. They'd gone about fifty yards from the bottom of the cliff when Gus saw it. Sitting under a sapling spruce was a shoe. A hiking boot, to be exact, turned on its side. Gus ran over. With a stick, he flipped the shoe right side up. Bloody bone and stringy tendons filled the inside. Gus ran away as fast as he could. Passing bits of torn clothes and a pile of bad guy guts. He closed his eyes, not wanting to look, but couldn't run with his eyes closed. He focused his sights straight ahead. Doing his best to not look down. Doing his best to stop seeing the dead guy being pulled apart and ate up by a bunch of hungry bears. Gus and Benny trotted out of there as fast as they could.

The duo hiked for three hours and covered six miles. Time and distance helped fade Gus's gory visions of what was left of Homer. Once he'd settled down, the realization came to mind that bears and buzzards had concealed his crime for him. If remains were ever found, they'd have to pin it on something other than him. Maybe Mother Nature was on his side. Maybe she knew what he was up against and wanted to help.

Traveling southwest the trail eventually merged onto an old logging road overgrown with weeds and deer brush. Gus was grateful to travel along mostly level and open ground. He was nearing the end of his hero's journey, his final mission. Mother Nature rewarded him and Benny with a brilliant sunset. The tangerine and lavender skyline made Gus feel good and fuzzy inside. Usually, the only time he ever felt this fuzzy inside was when he kissed Gloria, and he hoped this meant he was over her.

Mom was right like always. It began raining soon as they arrived at the hideout. A century-old abandoned mine —one of hundreds that scattered the gold country—that looked more like a long and narrow cave.

The entrance was an oval-shaped hole hidden in the hillside, secured with a rusted and ill-fitted iron gate for a door. Wired to the gate were two signs—NO TRESS-PASSING and a skull and crossbones that read Stay Alive Stay Out. Dense moss spread out above the opening like a lush sod roof. It reminded Gus of a hobbit hole, but not at all cheery and bright nor inhabited by a hobbit. He dug out the leather thong from around his neck and pulled it off over his head. The crucifix and the skeleton key dangled. Gus took a deep breath and worked the key into the old lock hanging from a heavy chain around the gate.

Gus's dad had shown him the mine years ago on a

fishing trip and warned him to never go inside due to the danger of collapse as he wrapped a chain through the gate and secured it with a lock as solid and sturdy as ore. That night, they had roasted hotdogs over a campfire outside the old mine, and Dad told the saga of Joaquin Murietta. The mine was Murietta's hideout for an entire winter after bandits had beaten him nearly to death, killed his wife and brother, then stole his gold. The mine mended and protected him from the outside world. Allowed him time to devise a vengeful rampage when he emerged.

The overweight gate screamed as Gus forced it open. The mine was dark but extremely dry and smelled rich—like gold. Gus adjusted his eyes and shook off his slicker then quickly found the headlamp in his coat pocket. He pulled it out, clicked it on, and unsaddled Benny just inside the door. His big ears pinned back and his head hung low because donkeys hate being wet more than anything.

The sweet smell of summer hung somewhere in the distance. Gus shined his light ahead and moved deeper and deeper down the shaft. Surrounded by carved-away earth and rock held by rotted timbers that moaned with a painful ache.

The mine was happy to see him again. It had been a dirty job, but Gus had cleaned and prepared the place two summers ago. At first, the creepy moans had spooked Gus, but he had a job to do and began negotiating. If the ghost of Joaquin Murietta wanted to scare him away, he could just forget it. Gus explained to the spirit that everyone, including him, admired what the Mexican bandit had done to those horrible miners who'd hurt his wife and brother for no good reason. It was exactly what good guys *should* do to bad guys, Gus explained, then apologized for disturbing Mr. Murietta's peace and quiet. He promised to hurry up and get out, if the ghosts would be quiet, leave him alone, and let him finish his job.

The spooky sounds and uneasy feelings settled down after Gus's bargaining with the underworld. In two days, he'd rolled all the fallen rocks outside, cleared sheets of cobwebs, and discovered a wooden box of explosives hidden behind a stack of rotting timbers in a tiny cavern off of the entrance. He knew better than to handle the sensitive stuff. Old dynamite had nitroglycerin in it that sweated over the years, causing it to become very unstable and easily combustible. Only an idiot or the bomb squad should touch it.

"Hola...Joaquin. Did you...miss me?" Gus whispered as he went deeper and deeper into the mine until the shaft forked. He followed the abrupt left further and further until he saw it. The result of an entire summer of hard work, sweat, and tears. Like a burlap weed train stuck in a tunnel. The shaft was stuffed wall to wall and top to bottom with burlap bundles of bud. Danny K. had transported a lot of weed. Gus inhaled the sweet, musty scent of success and smiled.

He made his way back to the entrance with a swing in his step and sat in the dirt. A gurgling growl alarmed him and he stiffened until realizing it was only his stomach. His jaw didn't hurt after eating the guts out of the salami and cheese sandwich. He fed the bread to Benny because bread needed moisture, like mayonnaise, or butter, or ranch dress-ing. The Search and Rescue sandwiches were bone dry and would clog his throat, plus he'd been trying to cut back on the carbs. Benny liked white bread, but wheat was his favorite. Gus gave him the wilted lettuce and mushy toma-toes too.

A campfire would have been nice. Something about the

movement of flames was relaxing, but he was plenty warm enough. Underground, the temperature was a perfect and constant sixty-five. Gus was smart enough to know that building a fire in a mine was a dumb idea, especially with all that weed and old dynamite.

Sick and tired of waiting, he unstrapped his bedroll, but did not unroll it. He just tossed it on the ground and rested his back against the soft canvas. Doing his best not to think of Gloria, he fell asleep.

In his dream, Gus could smell Gloria's grape gum as she chomped and tried to teach him how to blow a bubble. She blew a purple bubble so big that if it burst, it would have covered her entire face. She blew once more when it popped and Gus woke to Benny's bray. Before he could cover his ears, the heavy gate groaned open.

Gus sat up and pushed himself back and his bedroll up against a rotted timber. He snatched the gun out of his coat pocket as a light blinded him.

"Hey, buddy." Danny K. lowered his flashlight and corrected himself. "I mean *Joaquin.*" Danny K. laughed.

"Hola, Pancho." Gus stood and dusted himself off. He'd been so deep into his Gloria dream that he never heard Danny K. arrive. Although the mine wasn't far from the old logging road, only about a quarter mile uphill, Gus usually heard the quad coming.

"Here, I brought your favorite." Danny K. tossed a bag of Fritos in the air. Gus almost caught them before they hit the ground.

"Bad news, bud. Someone shot Homer," Danny K. said as Gus picked up the chips and set the bag on his bedroll. "I mean 'Omar'." Danny K. made air quotes. "I think his cranky girlfriend had something to do with it. They were stealing weed and I don't trust or like her."

Danny K. shook his head like he was trying to remove any and all doubt.

"Now she's gone. Just up and disappeared with a whole lot a product."

"Did you...tell Red?" Gus asked.

"Yes, and explained as best I could what happened yesterday and last night."

"What did he...say?" Gus tried not to sound too concerned.

"He was certainly livid and after all the cursing he said we should wait here until he feels it's safe."

"Okay...then...we'll wait."

"Yeah, I had a sneaking suspicion about that gal from the get go. I hate to tell you bud, but boy oh boy, it's not going to end well for her. I know how you feel about her and all, but—"

"It wasn't her. It was me." Gus admitted. "I stole...the weed."

"What do you mean?" Danny K. smiled and it took up most of his face. His big teeth eating through the dark.

"I...did it...I stole...the bundles...and I shot...Homer."

Danny K. guffawed. "No, you didn't. I know you, Gus. You're just trying to cover for her and it's not going to work. Red will never buy it for a second and neither will I. You need to accept the fact that Gloria is no good."

"You're...no good." Gus tightened his grip on the gun at his side. "No more...growing. The forest...has to heal... And bad...guys...have got to go."

"What are you talking about?"

"Walter!" Gus aimed his gun at Danny K. "And a calf. The forest...and the creek...got hurt because you...brought in bad pesticides! You did that!" Gus stepped forward and Danny K raised both hands. "Miss Mo...got hurt!"

"Whoa, August. Let's just take it easy. You're as much a part of this as anyone." Danny K. lifted his palms in surrender.

"No. I didn't...know...you'd poison...the water. And hurt animals. And people." Gus shook with anger. Thoughts banged in his head—erratic and scattered as dried leaves in the wind.

"You should *not* point guns at people unless you plan on using them."

"That's...the plan."

Danny K. tilted his head and set his hands on his breast. "But, Gus, I'm your pal. You don't want to hurt me."

"No...I don't, but the world... needs...*less*...bad guys. *You*...are...a...bad guy."

"I don't know what in the holy heck is going on in that kooky head of yours, but if Red finds out about this—" His nostrils flared. "Bottom line, bud, you shoot me, Red will put you in the barrel and roll you into the river along with your girlfriend. You've got a good thing going here. Don't screw it up."

"You...screwed...it up. Asshole!"

Danny K. stepped toward Gus and lifted his index finger. "Don't call me that." His kind face twisted. "You're starting to piss me off."

"I'm pissed off!" Gus pulled the trigger twice, and Danny K. fell with a satisfying thud.

Chapter Twenty-Six

Sleeping in a haunted mine was probably never easy, but sleeping with a dead guy nearby was pretty much impossible. Even though Gus had hidden Danny K. behind the burlap bundles with Benny's help, he remained in a state of wakeful sleep most of the night. Once, he'd fallen asleep but woke with a terrible fright when Benny pawed at the iron gate wanting out. Gus got up and opened it. The rain had let up and the instant Benny stepped outside, he stretched and peed. Gus did the same and considered removing a few more valuable bundles, but since there was no telling when Red would arrive, Gus couldn't risk it. If Red caught him with bundles of weed, he wouldn't wait for an explanation. Gus would be in a metal drum in the river just like Danny K. had said.

At four AM he thought of Murietta and how the man must have gone mad in the mine all winter long. Maybe madness is what it took to devise a good plan and follow through on it. Gus needed a plan. Not just any old plan, because Red was sharp. Shooting him would be the easiest way to rid the forest of another bad guy, but there was no way Red would be alone. He always had at least three or four guys with him, especially when doing business. That meant Gus would not only have to shoot Red—he'd have to shoot three or four other armed men without being shot himself. What if Red blamed him for the Gloria and Homer fiasco? Gus had vouched for Gloria. Oh God.

"Forget it." Gus gave up on sleep and strapped on his headlamp, munched a few handfuls of Fritos, when the idea struck like a match.

Gus jumped up and went to work. Moving the decaying box of dynamite was out of the question, so he had to be ingenious. Carefully, he lifted the dusty lid. Stringy cobwebs strained and busted away from the rotted rope handles. He stared down at the faded sticks stuffed in sawdust and layered in rows like fat cigars.

At daylight, Gus saddled and packed all his gear, minus the bedroll, back onto Benny. Once the gear was strapped down good and tight to the pack saddle, Gus led Benny one mile downhill by way of Danny K.'s quad. In a small section of dried grass, he stopped and removed Benny's packsaddle as the donkey grazed. Benny hadn't lifted his head once while Gus tied hobbles around his front legs, then shoved the packed gear deep into the manzanita bushes bordering the little pasture.

Gus rubbed Benny's neck. "I'll see...you later...buddy." He lifted Benny's lead rope, then his head, and kissed him on the nose. "Bye." Benny was too busy eating to worry about being left alone when Gus mounted Danny K.'s quad and drove away.

About a quarter of a mile below the old mine, Gus ditched the quad in a thicket. Tweakers would find it soon enough and after running it out of fuel they'd shoot holes in it and torch the thing. Gus plodded back to the mine and flopped onto his bedroll.

With all that had gone wrong because of Miss Mo and then the Homer thing, there was no telling when Red and his boys would arrive to pay him and transport the product on to the port of Stockton. But Gus was ready and waiting. Odds were good that they might not even know what all had happened. Odds were better than good that no one knew about Homer.

It was all he could do not to eat the rest of the Fritos and stop himself from obsessing over them. Gus laid down on top of his bedroll and made small talk with Joaquin until he got sleepy and drifted into a deep midmorning slumber.

Most of the day had come and gone unnoticed when Gus woke. Feeling rested, he stretched and yawned and smiled. Waiting was worse than being hungry and he couldn't stand how slowly the time passed. Doing nothing was boring and worse than hard work. He wanted so badly for this job to be over so he could go home and eat. He hoped like heck Mom's leftover meatloaf was in the fridge. Meatloaf covered in ketchup and an ice-cold glass of milk. He'd probably eat before taking a shower or anything else. Mom would sit with him while he ate, and he'd tell her that soon she would be moving out of the dumpy trailer and back to the ranch. Her smile would make all the bad stuff from the last few days, and the hunger, and the waiting, worth it.

Hibernating bats hung in a far corner of the mine and Gus wondered what it would be like to sleep for months upside down. He tried to stand on his head, using the earth wall as a brace and his bedroll to cushion his skull, but soon decided he was not built to be upside down and gave up.

Carving a heart with Gloria's name crossed out with an X into a flat spot on the granite wall wasted about an hour. When he was done, the Case pocketknife his father had given him when he turned sixteen was dull as a butter knife. The next hour was occupied by locating a smooth stone that fit nicely into his hand. He spit on the stone and worked the blade back and forth in a slow and steady motion until it was sharp.

Bored nearly to death, he threw his arms in the air and began jumping up and down for no good reason other than there was nothing else to do and he was sick of sitting around.

"What the fuck you doin' kid?" Red had arrived without a sound and came through the gate.

"Hi Red!" Gus approached him. "I was just...messing around. Waiting...for you."

"Good to see you."

They hugged and Gus didn't think he could go through with the plan. Red flipped his black hood down off a flame-colored pony tail. A copper and white beard spread across his chest like a fire.

Three guys filed in. The first guy was Sarge, who'd been working for Red longer than Gus. Sarge looked like a military man, with a spiky white crew cut and big muscles hidden under a green army coat.

The second guy was Brent or Brant, but Gus called him Bull because he wore boots and Wranglers and walked bowlegged on account of getting his leg broke in the bull riding at the Angels Camp rodeo four years ago. The third guy was Jordan Peterson. Gus hadn't liked him since third grade. He was nothing more than a punk who'd picked on anyone weaker than him in school and finally got his butt whipped in sixth grade. Gloria beat the crap out of him in front of everyone for calling Gus a retard. Maybe Gus could go through with the plan after all.

"Hey Shrek, where's Don-kay?" Jordan laughed like a donkey at his own sorry Scottish imitation of Shrek.

"Hi, Jordan." Gus wondered if maybe he was as big of a loser as Jordan since they both worked for Red.

Red glared at Jordan. "Wait outside."

Jordan went without a word, and Sarge grinned.

"Seen Dan?" Red asked.

"Not yet." Gus smiled his sweetest smile.

"I've got something for you." Red put one hand on Gus's shoulder and the other inside his heavy black jacket. He brought out a white envelope and handed it to Gus. "Since things got fuckin' sideways, and two farmers aren't going to be collecting their pay, I gave it to you. You earned it. But August, I need you to trust me from here on out. Okay?"

"Yes. Thanks…Red." Gus folded the thick envelope, tucked it into his coat pocket, and zipped the pocket shut. Relieved for a moment that Red wasn't blaming him for what had happened, until the sickening gut-punch that Gloria would pay with her life if Gus didn't stop him. He hated Gloria so much, but loved her more.

"Don't spend it all at once," Red instructed as Bull handed him a flashlight that lit the entire shaft as far down as Gus could see.

"I gotta go. Mom's got dinner…waiting." Gus pulled on his rain slicker.

"You wanna ride? Help us load and we'll take you down," Sarge offered.

"I have to...find Benny. He...wandered off...again." Gus rolled his bedroll, sweating profusely.

"You okay?" Bull asked.

Gus nodded and buckled the straps on his bedroll. "The bundles...are...in back."

"Yep. Okay. Good job, Gus. Tell your mom hello." Red walked away and the guys followed.

"Come on, Jordan," Sarge yelled and Jordan rushed in.

"Later, Slow Motion." Jordan whizzed by and Gus went as fast as he could in the opposite direction.

He hurried like never before behind the stacked timber to the box of explosives strategically covered in Fritos. Gus took a breath as he withdrew a wooden match from the box and struck it. The sharp smell of sulfur hung in the stagnant air as the match flared. He dropped the tiny flame into the sawdust. It disappeared without a spark.

"Crapola." Gus's hands shook as he removed a second matchstick and struck it. Heat singed his fingertips while he held the flame under a single Frito chip until the grease sizzled, then sparked, and burned like a mini torch. He placed the burning chip among the others and in a few seconds had himself a flaming grease fire that would ignite the underworld. Gus ran like his life depended on it because it did.

He wasn't sure how much time he had left and pushed through the heavy gate without his bedroll. He slammed it and ran the heavy chain through. It rattled inside his head as he pulled it around the gate as fast as he could. "Hurry!" The lock swung and it seemed impossible he'd live to eat meatloaf when the damn thing fell on the ground.

"Come on." Adrenaline kicked like a mule from the inside out.

A light moved inside the mine and caught the corner of

his eye. Someone was coming. Shit. He found the lock and strung both ends of the chain onto the clasp, and pinched it shut. "Yes." He ran.

"What are you doing?" Jordan yelled, but Gus didn't stop. Didn't look back. Jordan banged and shook and kicked the grate. "The little cocksucker locked us in! Hey!"

Gus moved his feet as fast as he could, shuffling straight downhill. The force from the blast shoved him like a bully from behind. He was mid-flight when a series of explosions blew the underground to hell. Rocks took flight like a flock of angry birds, falling dead from the sky all around him as he landed. Gus prepared to be pelted. He closed his eyes, covered his head with his hands, and tucked into a ball as tight as a pill bug. He waited and waited there on the ground. But it was over.

Gus opened his eyes and looked up. A plume of smoke clouded the sky. The air smelled like burnt cement. No longer burdened with humiliation, Gus got to his feet and dusted himself off. It was a terrible, awful thing that he'd done, but deep down inside it felt awesome. Saving the forest and ridding the world of corrupt and contaminated scumbags was like winning. As he headed home, it dawned on Gus that he might just have a knack for crushing bad guys, and he was ready to get on with his new career.

Chapter Twenty-Seven

Kate and I and Gus and the boys survived the entire pandemic without being infected by the dreaded virus. Fist-fights at the Dollar General over the mask mandate were a fading memory. February arrived with record-breaking snow and weeks of power outages. I'd fallen asleep early one evening as Kate massaged my feet and awoke sometime in the night when the power came on. The digital clock flashed twelve and Kate was not in bed. I got up and found her at the kitchen table pecking on my laptop with her index fingers. When I walked in, she slammed the lid down and said she was looking up cruise ship deals. I couldn't imagine Kate on a cruise if I'd kidnapped her. She'd be bored to tears unless someone bombed the ship.

The next morning, I opened the laptop and checked the browser's history. She'd been browsing local bakeries and researching vegan caterers. Life had bombarded me with lemons until I finally found the strength to ferment them into a magical lemonade elixir.

A week later, Kate took me, the twins, and Gus to a

birthday dinner at the historic and haunted Hotel Leger in Mokelumne Hill. When we arrived at home, Kate made sure I walked in the front door first. I acted surprised to see so many people crowded into our living room, yelling "Surprise!" Smiling and clapping as I brought my steepled fingers to my mouth. Being liked was more than I'd imagined. Their approval bordered on admiration and for the first time in my life I felt special. It was all due to the fact that Kate would prefer to be bullwhipped than entertain a houseful of guests. She put me first, before her own wants and needs. If that's not love, I don't know what is.

My kidnapping and ultimate survival made me the subject of local and national news. For once, a middle-aged woman won, beat the odds, and survived the evil in the world. I represented the ultimate underdog, became a new kind of hero, and suddenly had a birthday party and more friends than I could count. Kate hugged me.

"I love you," I whispered, kiss her cheek, and swallowed the lump in my throat.

Ed Manetti greeted me. "Happy Birthday, Mo." We hugged.

"Thank you, Ed. Really. I appreciate you coming."

"Are you kidding? I wouldn't miss it." He greeted Kate with a hug, then lifted Joey and Patrick at the same time. Kate never officially broke up with him because, according to her, there was nothing to break off. She explained to him how we planned to grow old together. Like a fairytale, Ed Manetti congratulated us and continued being a dear friend to both of us. When I asked him how he'd found the ability to be so gracious, he explained that he'd been through two ex-wives, the pandemic, and lawsuits that filled his life with more than enough drama. He simply didn't need or want anymore.

"If anyone deserves to be happy it's you two," he'd said and I believe he meant it.

Guests piled around the kitchen table and spilled out into the living room. With Joey in my arms and Patrick in Kate's, we waited patiently while Gus lit all fifty-five candles on my cake. Gretchen, Gus's mom wore a brilliant smile and kept her hand on his back until the last candle sparked.

"Pretty," Patrick said.

"Hope it tastes as good as it looks." Roper raised his brow.

"It's gluten free, so don't count on it." Kate rolled her eyes and laughter turned into the most glorious rendition of "Happy Birthday" I'd ever heard. For a few hours, my life was as good as it gets, and I appreciated it. I also couldn't shake the feeling that it wouldn't last.

The moment Gus asked me to come into his room, I suspected the worst.

Walter slept peacefully on Gus's bed. His ear had healed beautifully. The veterinarian sutured the split and in a few weeks the flaps grew together, leaving only a scar that could be felt more than seen.

"Happy Birthday...Miss Mo." Gus hugged me, then shut the bedroom door and handed me a gift bag.

"Thank you." I untied the red ribbon and looked into the bag. "Your wrapping skills exceed mine," I said and dug through the tissue paper, down to something of substance.

"My new...girlfriend...helped me."

"What?" I looked at him. "Gus, you didn't tell me you're seeing someone. Who is she?"

"Her name...is...Mia. She...just moved here...from... Lake Tahoe. She loves...animals too...and is going to... teach me...how to...snowboard."

"Gus, that's fantastic. I can't wait to meet her."

"She is…an older…woman…by two years." Gus smiled. "My mom…is bringing her over tonight…after work."

"I'm thrilled for you, Gus." I buried my hand in the gift bag and pulled out a black and orange San Francisco Giants cap exactly like the one I'd lost at Forest Creek. "Wow. This is—very thoughtful. Thank you."

"I found it…at Forest Creek. You had it on…when I saw you…fishing. I wasn't sure…you'd want it back…but Mia… said…you would."

"I appreciate it." I buried the cap back in the bag, refusing to let thoughts of the man who'd stolen it from me intrude on my good time. "Thank you."

"Grammy Kate…told me…you sold your book."

"Yes."

Jessica Williams, the bestselling local author, had been hired to ghostwrite *The Magic Outside Your Comfort Zone*, which my agent retitled *Fueled by Fear*, and included how I'd survived Forest Creek. A bidding war between three of the big publishing houses broke out and within forty-eight hours, I had signed an NDA and a contract worth more than I could have imagined. The first part of my advance was large enough to purchase the old bar on Main Street where I planned to open a free behavioral health center for the community. I donated fifty thousand dollars to the Calaveras County animal shelter. A patient gifted a huge painting of Walter and me, which now hangs in the lobby.

After a media frenzy and an interview on Dr. Phil's podcast, donations from around the country poured into my favorite environmental non-profits for the cleanup of toxic waste left by illegal cannabis cultivation in our National Forests. In only five months, I had made the positive impact on the world I'd always dreamed of.

"Some good has come from of all of the bad that happened." I unconsciously shrugged and touched my throat.

"Grammy Kate...says...I'm something good...that came...from something bad." Gus looked up at me with tears in his eyes.

"You are." I sat next to him on the bed and put my hand on his shoulder. "What's bothering you?"

"Do you...think...liars...are bad?"

I flinched. An involuntary kind of knee-jerk reaction struck me like a mallet. I considered his question carefully. Searching for an intelligent yet realistic answer. "To tell you the truth, I believe it depends on the individual situation."

Gus stood up and held my hand. "I know...the truth... Miss Mo."

My stomach lurched. "Truth about what, Gus?"

He let go of my hand, and I wiped my sweaty palms along my thighs. Time stood still as muffled sounds of idle chit-chat and laughter reminded me the party and the world would go on without me.

"Forest Creek."

I couldn't speak—trying my best to untangle the thoughts morphing into mouth-watering nausea. The fear I'd endured at Forest Creek had found me once again.

"I won't tell. People say...your story...helped them...to be strong...and better. A lady...at my church...said... because of you...her daughter quit drugs...and she got her...kids back. I don't want to...ruin it. But...I know... only some...of your story...is true. The man...you called Omar...is Homer. He was...Gloria's boyfriend. He told me...you got scared...and ran...and fell...and they saved you." Gus's shoulders slouched and he looked straight through me.

"No. That's not true. He hit me with something." This part of my story I'd believed happened. A double knot hit the bottom of my stomach. "You know this man? You spoke to him?"

Gus nodded. "You fell."

"But I heard him shoot Walter. I saw the man. He pointed a gun at me!" That was no hallucination. It was the middle of the day and my hallucinations only occurred upon waking. "I ran." Talking to Kate over the phone while running for my life. Screaming for help. Gasping for my next breath—trying not to fall. "I fell."

Gus nodded. "Yes."

"The man didn't hit me in the head?" I was slipping under water. About to drown.

"No." Gus gently set his hand on my shoulder. "You… hit your own head…when you fell. You…would have…died if they left you…out…in the woods…all night."

I sat up straight, exhaled with great drama, and nodded as the events at Forest Creek played in my mind like my hallucinations. Jagged pieces coming together and forming a fragmented picture.

I covered my mouth. My chest tightened as the nausea clawed its way up my throat.

"It's okay…sometimes head injuries…cause memory loss. Maybe…you forgot." Gus waited for an answer I didn't have. "Maybe…you were…just confused."

I was confused alright, now more than ever, certain beyond all doubt the man or someone had hit me with something.

Gus's eyes darted around the room as if someone who shouldn't be might be listening. "At camp, you were…tied up…the whole time."

This I knew, and picked and pulled at a hangnail on my

thumb until it bled. Avoiding eye contact. Unable to find the words to make him understand why I'd lied.

"Where's this coming from? How do you know all this? Do you know these criminals?" My heart throbbed as I wiped my bleeding thumb on my pants.

"Yes." Gus nodded. "Lupe...was...my Gloria. She promised me...they never hurt you. You...didn't escape. Your eyes...were covered...but the tape...came off. You saw Danny K...when he...came to haul...weed out. Then Gloria...put more...tape...over your eyes."

"Gloria is Lupe? You spoke to her? Gus, she belongs in jail."

"She...is done...being bad. She is...going...to be a... dental hygienist."

"The man, Omar, and Gloria saved me?"

"Homer is his...real name."

"Homer? Homer, is Omar—" I dropped my head in my hands and put it together. I had truly believed the man was chasing me.

"They used...fake names. Gloria...got them...from... her favorite book...*Blue Mountain*. Remember...Lupe...and Omar...were bad guys...who were...never seen."

Gloria and Homer were not Hispanic after all. Had I been influenced and made assumptions of their ethnicity based off numerous news reports of the cartel growing cannabis in the National Forest? Had I secretly harbored an underlying racism buried deep in my marrow years ago due to the abuse I'd endured from Rosemary Rivera? A Hispanic.

"Homer." The recollection came rushing back clear as could be and was not part of my hallucination. I was sure of it. Gloria, also known as Lupe, had said that someone had shot Homer. "Homer." His name lingered in the silence. "Homer Lipinski?"

"Yes."

I looked up at Gus as he stood in front of me. "His brother is Deputy Lipinski? They're looking for him."

"Homer...is a bad...guy."

"He's missing. He and Danny Kilpatrick."

"They're gone." Gus smiled down at Walter and petted his head.

"Do you know where?"

He shrugged. "Miss Mo, did...you want...to be famous?"

"No! Absolutely not." I shook my head. "This has nothing to do with notoriety." The sound of a diesel truck warming up came from outside. People were beginning to leave. "Gus, please understand, most of my career has been spent with a front-row seat to the atrocities of life. I just wanted to balance the scales a little. To make a difference in the world and do something truly impactful before I die."

"Me too." Gus smiled. "I think we did." Gus sat on the foot of the bed next to me. "Good guys...are winning."

I looked at him and took a deep breath. "Gus, listen I'd like to explain. Okay?"

Gus nodded, "Okay."

"I suffer from something called hypnopompic hallucinations. You know what that is?"

He thought a moment, "Like Russell Crowe...in that movie...*A Beautiful Mind?*"

"I don't know the film, but—"

"It's about...John Nash. He won the...Nobel Prize...in economics...and he had...hallucinations."

"Ahh, yes, I'm familiar with his illness. But this is different. My hallucinations only happen upon waking. It's been happening since childhood and finally caught up with me while tied to that tree. I was terrified, Gus. And exhausted. My head felt like it was going to explode. I just wanted to close my eyes and sleep, but suspected I likely had a concussion. I knew not to fall asleep, but there came a point I could no longer hold my eyes open. Once I woke, my daring escape hallucinations began."

"Whoa." He looked at the ceiling and back and forth like he was confused yet amazed.

"Gus, when you found me, I was extremely grateful, but as my rescue progressed, the scenario planted earlier by the prolonged hallucinations began to grow. Then the idea of inspiring people with a few simple lies hit and immediately outweighed my conscience until what was real no longer mattered."

"Well...it *is* a...good story. But, I'm...glad...Gloria didn't...shoot at you. And...Homer did not try to...you know...get on top of you."

I sighed as the weight of my lies shifted with his understanding.

"You...would have drowned...if you fell...in the river... or froze to...death. It was...too cold."

"Probably. But you never know. A strong mind matters more than skill or brute strength in a survival situation."

"If you think you can...or you think...you can't...you're right," Gus said. "You...told me that."

"It's true."

Gus seemed to take my words into consideration as he crossed his arms and looked at his feet. The need to fill the silence felt like a burden.

"I refused to speak with the detectives at the hospital. The doctor agreed that I'd been severely traumatized and instead of being interviewed, I wrote my entire story down.

Scene by scene, play-by-play, and gave it to Grammy Kate to take to the sheriff's department."

"Does...Grammy Kate know...the truth?"

"I think she suspects something's off, but no. She doesn't know." The thought of Kate's disappointment at learning I was a liar caused my face to flush. It's not possible to retreat into a bottomless pit, one can only plunge. I stood and felt myself falling.

Gus went to the window and slid it open. The icy air cooled my anxiety as I took in deep breaths. Gus watched me.

"If you love...Grammy...you have...to tell her...the truth."

"I know." I sucked in the deepest breath I could. "I know. I'd planned to tell her the day we came home from the hospital. I was ready to retract the entire story until Jessica Williams called and explained what an underdog hero I'd become and how my survival could be huge. Grammy Kate was so proud of me. The way she looked at me was wonderful. I—" Tears came and ran down my face as I swallowed my guilt.

"The better my lies became the better the story became." I shook my head and closed the window. "Struggle is what gives life value. Do you understand that?" I focused on Walter's ear and sat down next to him on the bed.

"I guess." Gus shrugged like he did not care rather than comprehend what I was trying to explain.

Trying to convince Gus and obtain his approval, I rubbed Walter's scarred ear and did my best. "Struggle in life is the same for a story. I had valuable information I wanted to share with readers. To inspire and show them how different life could be once they faced their fears. To crack open the door of possibility. But no one would have cared, Gus. No one would listen unless I grabbed them around the throat and gave them a damn good reason. My story of surviving the odds digs deep into the psyche and motivates readers to believe they too can accomplish anything—including change for the better—they just have to believe it's possible." That was the truth. I had sold my soul for the betterment of humanity.

Gus chewed his lower lip. He was on the fence, unable to decide if my behavior was acceptable or not. I loved and admired him. I craved his understanding as to why I lied.

"Do you know how many letters I've received in the last few months from people who've heard my story? They say it gave them the strength to do things they never thought possible. I know it was wrong, Gus, but weighed against the outcome I'd say it was a lie worth telling."

Gus crossed his arms and looked down at me. "You got a lot...of money...for a lie."

"Yes. And I'm not keeping any of it. Every cent will be spent on improving *other* people's lives."

"And animals too...right?" He was remarkably kind.

"Yes. Many animals will benefit. They have benefited. I've donated fifty thousand dollars to the animal shelter."

Then he blasted me with both barrels.

"Will you help...my sanctuary?" A wistful grin grew on Gus's face and carried with it every characteristic but innocence.

"That's a *wonderful* idea." I stood up and hugged him. "I'd be glad to help."

"I need...a lot," Gus said into my shoulder as he squeezed me.

"Whatever it is we'll get it. I promise. We'll begin a task list and create a financial plan first thing tomorrow. Okay?"

"Thank you…Miss Mo." He released his hold on me and clapped his hands. "Yes!" He pumped his fists over his head. "Thank you."

I looked into his eyes unsure if I'd tainted his innocence with my deception or just been manipulated by a very clever young man. Everyone, including me, had underestimated him. This would take a lifetime to dissect, analyze, and comprehend, but for now, all I could do was laugh. I couldn't stop myself and laughed like a lunatic until Gus laughed too.

The truth would unravel eventually. Sooner or later, I'd accept my penance, confess my sins, and my story would sell to an entirely new audience of believers. My publishers would likely sue, but so what? Their money would be gone for good. The greater good.

More by Lisa Michelle

vinci-books.com/calaverascrimeseries

Follow the link to stay up to date with Lisa Michelle's new releases

Acknowledgments

Thank you dear reader. Without you, my work would not exist.

Thank you to my well-versed read team, Pat Russell, Frank Riley, Tim Hauserman, Paula DiFalco, Chelle Northcutt, Lillian Schneider, Don Urbanus, Marissa Taylor, Dawn Crikman, and Tahoe Writers Works. These folks suffered through early drafts of *Forest Creek*, but convinced me that the cast of quirky characters were compelling enough to follow anywhere.